GRUMPY PUCK

MISHA BELL

♠ MOZAIKA PUBLICATIONS ♠

Copyright © 2024 Misha Bell
www.mishabell.com

Published by Mozaika Publications, an imprint of Mozaika LLC.
www.mozaikallc.com

Cover by Najla Qamber Designs
www.qamberdesignsmedia.com

ISBN: 978-1-63142-921-7
Paperback ISBN: 978-1-63142-939-2

CHAPTER 1
CALLIOPE

I stare into the bathroom mirror. The insane eyes of a killer clown/plush bear hybrid glare back at me from underneath giant red spectacles.

"All right, Calliope," I tell myself. "Time to get into character." Creasing my brow, I growl, "Bearman angry. Bearman want honey—the sweet nectar, the poo of bee, not big-breasted Pookie-poo. Roar. Now Bearman want a piece of Pookie-poo's ass."

Under the clown-bear's head, Wolfgang's tiny toes reassuringly massage my scalp. I grab a rat pellet from my jean pocket and sneak it into my headgear.

Yes, I brought one of my pet rats to this new job. No, I haven't learned my lesson, not even after being banned from every theme park in Orlando for getting caught rat-handed.

But how could I not let Wolfgang tag along? He gets terrible separation anxiety whenever I leave without him.

A toilet flushes, which I take as my cue to leave the bathroom and go in search of the ice rink.

Wherever that is.

Maybe I should have asked the HR lady? Or the coach?

This arena is enormous, way bigger than what I imagined a Florida hockey team would have. I wander down one hallway after another before coming across a beefy dude who reminds me of a kangaroo.

"Excuse me," I say. "Which way is the ice rink?"

He tells me, but when I follow his directions, I end up in a chlorine-scented room where the water is still in liquid form.

"Do you think ice rinks are pools when they're not sufficiently cold?" I ask Wolfgang.

As usual, I can picture his reply. It comes in a professorial tone with a heavy German accent:

Meine Liebe, the energy required to freeze such a large body of water would be astronomical. That electricity would be much better spent running pumps attached to a million cow teats so that the resulting milk could be turned into a billion bliss-filled cubes of cheddar.

I sigh. It seems like I might have to get my phone out and call—

Do I hear a pack of hyenas behind me?

"Mr. Bloom!" someone shouts loudly before I can turn. "Are you ready for your swim?"

Mr. Bloom?

Wait a second. That's the name of the mascot, which means—

Someone pushes me from behind.

Shit. My furry arms flail like those of a scarecrow in a hurricane, and then I fall right into the pool.

Splash.

Adrenaline spiking, I rip the bear's head off of me to make sure Wolfgang can swim freely. Then I spit out the nasty pool water that got into my mouth.

"What the fuck?" says a menacing, growly voice from dry land. "That isn't Ted."

Does he mean the guy I replaced? Shouldn't everyone here know that he's missing? Then again, maybe not. The coach did swear me to secrecy.

There's a huge splash, and then a big, sexily hairy arm wraps around my waist under the water.

Okay. This is a rescue. Thank goodness.

I grab Wolfgang from where he's scrambling to stay afloat and allow the arm owner to drag me out of the pool and set me down onto my feet.

"She's dripping everywhere. Get her out of the suit," says the kangaroo-looking guy who misled me with the directions. He's one of several beefy dudes who are standing by the pool room's entrance, clearly having snuck up behind me.

"Touch her, and I'll break your fingers," says the gruff voice of my savior.

"That's pretty violent," I say, turning to check out the speaker.

And... wow.

He's shirtless and muscled like a god. His face is fierce, angular, and almost perfectly symmetrical, except for his aristocratic nose, which seems to have been broken at some point and then healed slightly imperfectly—which only highlights the perfection of everything else.

He slowly examines me through a pair of somber eyes that are darker than the inside of a black hole.

Oh, boy.

There's stubble on his cheeks that I want to reach out and touch.

But I don't.

If I were going to be inappropriate, I'd touch the thick hair on his naked chest instead. Body hair is my sexual kryptonite when it comes to men, and even now, cold and embarrassed, I find myself wet in more ways than one.

"Are you okay?" he asks in that growly voice of his, then tucks a wet strand of my hair behind my ear.

Oh. My. Fucking. God. His touch is like the sting of an electric eel… right on my clit. And nipples. And—

"Call a fucking ambulance," my savior growls at the kangaroo guy. "Do it fast, and maybe I won't kill you for tricking me into pushing her."

Wait…

"You pushed me?" I glare up at his ridiculously handsome face.

"It was a misunderstanding," the guy retorts. "I thought you were Ted, and that one"—he gestures at either the kangaroo guy or one of the other muscle-bound dudes—"told me that Ted called me a—"

"Look, Michael," Kangaroo says conspiratorially. "Ted did call you—"

"I'm not Ted." I snatch my bear's head from where it's floating near the edge of the pool and watch with jealousy as Wolfgang scrambles up my arm to my shoulder and expertly shakes off his wet fur.

The asshole—Michael—narrows his dark eyes at my little friend. "Is that a rat?"

"No, it's a giraffe." I turn on my heel and trudge away with squelching sounds.

"Fucking fuck," Michael growls. "Hold up."

"Let me help you with those wet clothes!" Kangaroo shouts.

"Do not mention her clothes again." Michael's growl turns threatening. "Not if you want to keep the little marbles that pass for your balls."

"So you've checked out his balls?" I say over my shoulder and immediately wish my oldest brother were here.

He'd have a pair of sponge balls appear out of thin air and would label my words a "mad burn."

"Will you slow the fuck down?" Michael grumbles, falling into step next to me. "Where do you think you're going?"

"The ice rink." Wherever that is.

"It's cold there. You'll catch your death. At least change first."

"Yeah, into what?"

Apparently, when Ted disappeared, the backup mascot suit, along with all of his worldly possessions, went missing from his apartment.

Correction, *my* new apartment.

Yep. One of the main perks of this job is a rent-free

place to crash, so I don't have to live with the literal circus that is my family.

"I can help," Kangaroo says, trotting after us. "Find some clothes, that is."

Michael's growl goes polar. "What did I just say, Jack? This is your last warning."

Kangaroo Jack? I could swear my grandma was recently watching a movie with that exact title while rehearsing her tightrope-walking routine.

"I'm supposed to meet the team," I explain without stopping. "The coach told me they're about to finish practice at the rink."

He also said that this first week is a probationary period, and that I'll lose the job if I mess up. Or if Ted shows up with a "miraculously good excuse for his vanishing act."

"You've already met the team," Michael informs me. "Remember the morons by the pool?"

Oh. Great. I turn and face him. "Present company included?"

He frowns. "I'm on the team, but few people call me a moron and—"

"You're a moron," I say.

Kangaroo Jack's eyes widen.

"I pushed you, so I'll ignore that this time," Michael growls through teeth clenched so tightly their enamel is in big trouble. "Come back tomorrow. If our coach asks, we'll all say—"

"Fine." Wolfgang would appreciate a session under a hair dryer. "It was not a pleasure to meet you."

Unless we count his touch, that is, and the feast my eyes enjoyed until I learned what kind of a man he is.

Michael's jaw tightens further. "The lack of pleasure was mutual, I assure you."

"Those are not real sayings," Kangaroo Jack complains.

"Go to the dick!" Michael snaps at him.

As far as I know, that's not a saying either—but I like it and may use it on my youngest sister the next time she tries to show me one of her cringy contortionist pretzel poses.

I keep walking, ignoring the men trailing after me, and soon reach the small closet that was assigned to me as a dressing room. Before I can step inside, I notice that someone helpfully left a tall, skinny mirror right outside the door, sparing me from having to run to the bathroom the next time I suit up.

My reflection makes me wince. I look like a sad, soggy bear who's just eaten a similarly wet clown… and now his tummy hurts.

Unable to help myself, I get into character. "Roar. Bearman so mad. Bearman wet, like pussy."

There's such a loud gasp from Kangaroo Jack that I half expect him to swoon when I whip around to check what's wrong.

Wow. For some unknown reason, Michael is staring at me with such menace on his face you'd think I drowned his puppy, ate his kitten, and stuck his lucky puck up my butt.

"Do you know what happened to the last person who mocked him like that?" Kangaroo Jack exclaims in horror. Shooting a nervous glance at Michael, he informs me shakily, "He lost four teeth."

"Shut the fuck up," Michael growls.

"Oh, right. It wasn't four," Kangaroo Jack says, backing away from Michael as if he were radioactive. "It was seven."

CHAPTER 2
MICHAEL

"What are you talking about?" The mascot girl protectively clutches the rat to her chest—like I'd ever hurt a woman or a small animal.

A flare of pain in my jaw makes me realize I've clenched my teeth too hard… again. I can't help but glare at her. "Are you playing stupid now?"

Everyone knows I hate being called a bear. It's something I've had to deal with since childhood, thanks to the deadbeat parents I've never met. Before abandoning me, they gave me two dubious gifts: the last name "Medvedev" and first name "Mikhail," or "Misha" for short. Medvedev straight-up translates to "of bear" from Russian, and Misha is also associated with fucking bears—thanks to another fucking mascot, that of the Moscow Olympic Games. Oh, and when I moved to the US, things only got worse because Russians in general are associated with bears. Not to mention, I'm on this fucking team, which—

"Did you just call me stupid?" The girl's pretty green eyes narrow into tiny slits.

"I didn't, but I could," I tell her. "After all, it's stupid to poke the bear."

Fucking fuck. I just called myself a bear, didn't I?

"Yeah, he hates it when anyone calls him a bear," Jack explains warily, and the only reason I don't knock him the fuck out is because I don't want to scare the girl… any more than I already have, that is.

"I wouldn't even mention bears in his proximity," Jack continues. "We don't even offer him beer, in case—"

"Wait." She blinks at each of us with long and distractingly feminine eyelashes. "Your team is called the Florida *Bears*."

The only reason I don't bare my teeth at her—or at anyone—is that doing so will only bring about further comparisons to fucking bears. "The team was called the Orlando Blooms when I got drafted." And now I'm fucking stuck with them.

"Wow. That was a terrible name." She examines the clown-bear head of the mascot that I hate so fucking much. "That at least explains why this one is called Mr. Bloom."

"Anything is better than the current name," I grit out. Even Mother Puckers would be an improvement. Or Ass Puckers. Or Bloomin' Onions.

Everyone shakes their heads, seemingly even the rat.

"We're not even in Orlando," the mascot chick says.

"We could just be the Florida Blooms then," I counter.

"There's also that actor," she says.

I clench and unclench my fists. "Fuck him."

"I don't think he'd want to fuck me," she says wistfully.

The surge of jealousy streaking through my veins is as surprising as it is unwelcome. I have no idea what's come over me. Side bar: the actor would have to be a eunuch to not want to fuck this girl. True, her body is hidden by the hideous suit, but she's tall and has a strikingly pretty face. With her pink hair, rosy cheeks, and delicate neck, she reminds me of a flamingo. And flamingoes are one of the few things I like about this fucking state. Maybe the only things.

She's so pretty, in fact, that I can almost forgive her for calling me a fucking Bearman. Especially since I *did* push her into the pool.

"You know what?" I say magnanimously. "We're even now."

"Just like that?" Jack stares at me like I've sprouted feathers.

"Excuse me." The girl straightens her spine, which is when I realize just how tall she is—the top of her head is almost to my chin. "When I hurt your delicate feelings, I was actually getting into character, not taunting anyone. How does that compare with you pushing me into the pool *on purpose*?"

"Getting into character?" Jack and I ask in unison.

"Yeah." She lifts the bear's head in front of her and says in an exaggeratedly growly voice, "Bearman angry. Bearman has a female inside of him, instead of the other way around."

My teeth clench involuntarily again. "Like I said, I didn't push *you*. It was a misunderstanding." I glare at Jack, who wisely steps outside my punching and kicking range. I turn my attention back to the girl. "You, on the other hand, just mocked me on purpose. Again."

"No. Bearman is Mr. Bloom." She waves the mascot head in front of me. "Mr. Bloom isn't you… right?"

"Then call your invisible friend Mr. Bloom when you get into character," I grit out. "Or better yet, don't get into character when I'm within earshot."

She bares her teeth—which doesn't make *her* look the least bit bearlike. Probably because said teeth are small, white, and very pretty. "I have an even better idea," she hisses. "How about we don't speak to each other at all? Ever."

I fight the urge to straight-up growl at her. "That's fine by me." I turn on my heel. "Let's go, Jack."

As Jack tags along, he looks reluctant—which nearly costs him some teeth.

I wait until we're out of the mascot's earshot before I declare to Jack, "She's off limits."

He looks taken aback. "To date, or play pranks on?"

"Off limits." I imbue the words with a promise of castration. "Spread the word."

Jack clears his throat. "You know the team has a hazing ritual. Mascot or not, she's on the team and is a newbie…"

"Fucking fuck." Those assholes can be fast, too. My first day, those fuckers stole my clothes and left the mascot costume in their stead. I don't know what the fuck they expected would happen, but I left the locker room naked and three of them ended up in the emergency room.

What the fuck are they going to do to *her*?

"Where are those fuckers?" I ask furiously, and when he says he doesn't know, I go in search of the rest of the team.

————

I locate them outside the main entrance to the arena, so I tell them to fucking listen to the words I'm about to say very carefully, like their health depends on it. I then explain that no pranks are allowed when it comes to the new mascot.

"But everyone gets pranked on their first day," whines Isaac, our so-called captain.

I grab him by the collar of his shirt and lift him off his feet. "Except her. Is that clear?"

"Actually, these idiots have already set their prank in motion," says Dante, our goalie, who's the most competent player and the closest thing to a friend I have on this fucking team.

Oh, and if our league allowed the goalie to be team captain, he'd be ours, and not the ass wipe that I'm currently holding. This guy can't even spell the word "leader."

Releasing Isaac, I turn to Dante. "Already?"

Dante runs his vampire-pale hand through his jet-black hair. "Everyone in the building is about to get a cell phone alert instructing them to evacuate."

As if on cue, my phone dings, and the message is

exactly what Dante said it would be: some bullshit about a gas leak.

My molars clench tight again. "I take it the girl is not getting this message?"

A bunch of them shake their heads.

My gaze zeroes in on Isaac. "And what happens next?"

"Nothing bad," Isaac says, cringing. "As part of the emergency protocol, all the doors will automatically lock. But they'll reopen tomorrow."

I'm not sure how, but Isaac ends up dangling in my fist again. "She's soaking wet from the pool fiasco, and you're about to lock her in an air-conditioned building?"

"It wasn't my idea," Isaac says.

What a motherfucker. Disgusted, I let go of him and scan the guilty-looking mugs surrounding me. "Whose fucking idea was it then?"

"Jack's," they say in unison.

"What?" My fists clench as I spin to face Jack. "You were with me this whole time."

Jack backs up, paling. "I came up with it before you said she was off limits. The janitor helped. I can call him to reset the system sooner, or—"

"How long before the doors lock?" I snap.

"Five minutes."

I turn toward the arena just as the first members of the staff exit. "You all had better pray I make it in time."

CHAPTER 3
CALLIOPE

"The nerve of that guy." I set Wolfgang onto the little table in my makeshift dressing room.

His beady eyes glint, as though with wisdom.

Meine Liebe, men like that need to unwind in pine forests, take warm baths, and eat copious amounts of cheese.

"Great. Now I have a mental image of Michael, naked, roaming the forest for honey… and then relaxing in a warm stream."

Wolfgang rubs his front paws on his face, like my dirty thoughts have made him feel unclean.

"Whatever." I scout the little room for something dry that I can wear.

Dusty magazines. Nope.

Expired Gatorade. Nope.

A pile of hockey jerseys. Score.

Stripping down to nothing, I utilize a few of them as the worst towels ever, then put on the largest one, which happens to be the number eight.

Okay. The jersey is scratchy and way too baggy, but it covers all of my girl parts, so it might just work.

I take a few steps and cringe. Going commando like this will suck. Maybe I'm better off wearing wet undies than none?

Someone knocks on the door so loudly Wolfgang squeaks and leaps off the table onto my arm before scurrying up to my shoulder.

"Who's there?" I yell.

"Michael," a familiar voice growls in a very bear-like manner. "Come out. Quickly."

I approach the door but do not open it. "I'll come out when I'm good and ready." And when I have underwear on.

"Do I need to break this fucking door?"

"Didn't we just decide not to talk to each other?" Despite my combative words, I use a soothing tone that Grampa taught me. He trained lions, but his techniques work on rats as well, so I figure a bear shouldn't be that different.

"Fucking fuck," he growls. "Can we start the not-talking after I get you out of this fucking building?"

Curiosity runs in my family, so I can't help but open the door a crack. "Why are you getting me out of the building?"

"My stupid teammates are playing a prank on you as we speak," he grits out. "In five minutes, all the doors in this fucking place will lock."

Shit. "Why didn't you say so from the start?"

"I thought telling you to come out quickly would be enough."

The only reason I don't argue is the lack of time.

I open the door fully. "Lead the way."

He looks me up and down with a strange expression, then takes off down the corridor with ground-eating strides. Despite my longer-than-average legs, I have to jog to catch up, clutching Wolfgang to make sure he doesn't fall from my shoulder. I don't jog fast enough, apparently, because he stops at the first turn and glares at me. "Don't you understand the concept of hurry?"

"I'm practically sprinting," I huff. In fact, I ran out of the dressing room in such a rush that I'm barefoot. I also completely forgot to resolve the underwear question, and now I feel a draft on my nether regions, made all the worse by the dampness caused by Michael's T-shirt clinging to his powerfully muscled back.

On my shoulder, Wolfgang chirps.

Meine Liebe, I usually prefer females, and rats at that, but even I have to agree—this man looks gouda.

"What the fuck is 'practically' running?" Michael demands. "Run like you don't want to be stuck in this building all night."

Not willing to admit out loud that he has a good point, I start actually running, and Michael picks up his own pace until we're sprinting down the corridors and leaping down the stairs two at a time.

Despite the haste, just as we get to the doors that are our destination, something dings, and the stupid things lock right in front of our noses.

"Fucking fuckers." Michael slams a fist into the door —to no avail. He then starts talking in tongues, or rather one specific tongue that sounds familiar to what's spoken in Cold War-era movies.

"Are you cursing in Russian?" I guess.

He stops his soliloquy. "What other language would a guy with the last name Medvedev curse in?"

I roll my eyes. "I didn't even know your last name."

"Oh." He takes a breath and exhales slowly, then extends his hand. "I'm Michael Medvedev."

I know it would be smart—albeit rude—to ignore the proffered hand. However, something possesses me to shake it.

Wow. His grip is firm, and his palm is deliciously callused. And warm. And strong.

The zing to my clit is even stronger this time—for which I blame my lack of panties.

With effort, I let go of his hand and pull myself together. "I'm Calliope Klaunbut," I say, pronouncing my last name as "claw-un-boot." "And, as I said before, it is *not* a pleasure to meet you."

"The lack of pleasure is still mutual." He turns back toward the door and slams his fist into it again.

"Try your head," I suggest.

He whirls on me. "Why are you so fucking calm? Don't you realize we're stuck here?"

"What do you expect me to do?"

He looks me up and down. "Worry about catching a cold or hypothermia?"

Actually, despite my lack of clothes, I feel hot… and bothered, but I'm not going to tell him that. "Is there a supply closet or something here where I can get more clothes?" I ask instead.

"One second." He turns toward the door and beats on it so fiercely I half expect it to crack open.

But no. The heavy door takes the abuse in stride.

Michael turns back to me, looking like a bear who's failed to catch a delicious salmon.

"If it makes you feel any better," I say, not sure why I'm trying to reassure the asshole, "that looks like it's built to withstand a hurricane."

He grunts something unintelligible in response before turning on his heel and storming off in the direction we came from.

Wolfgang and I exchange a glance.

Meine Liebe, do you think he'll brie back?

With a shrug, I follow the bear—and have to resort to running yet again to keep up. Which is why when Michael stops suddenly on the second floor, I run smack into him.

It's like hitting a wall of pure, sexy muscle.

"In here." He gestures at the door in front of us.

I check the sign above it. "The team's locker room?"

"They aren't in there." He opens the door and holds it expectantly.

Oh, well.

I step inside, and the first thing I notice is the musky —but not completely unpleasant—smell of sweaty men. The second thing I notice is the huge mess.

"Now what?" I ask. "You expect me to steal something from your teammates?"

If he suggests I grab some of the dirty underwear lying about, I'm going to smack him.

"No stealing." He walks up to some sort of a

contraption. "This machine is meant to squeeze out moisture from swimwear. You can use it to get your own clothes dry."

Huh. "Wait here."

I rush back to my dressing room and come back with my stuff.

"Look away," I order him.

"Why?" he growls.

"Because I'm about to dry some unmentionables."

Did he just turn away too swiftly? What did he expect to see, horror-movie granny panties?

Whatever. I stick my undies into the machine and press the button.

The thing sounds like a starving hippopotamus as it does whatever it does. Afterward, I check my panties.

Nope. Still too damp to wear comfortably.

Fuck.

I run the thing again—and get the same result.

I pull out my phone from the pocket of my jeans and thank goodness that it's waterproof. I then test the machine on the jeans, and it works out a tiny bit better, in that they go from soaking wet to unpleasantly damp.

Hmm. "No luck," I tell Michael's back. I bite my lip, debating, then decide to go for it. "Do you happen to have a brand-new pair of underwear?"

His shoulders tense, and for a moment, I think he might snap at me. Instead, he walks to the locker with a large number eight written on it and rummages inside. Facing me, he hands me a pair of men's briefs and a sweater, then turns around.

I put on the briefs. Interesting. "They fit me perfectly," I tell him. And can I hope I'll be less turned on now that I've hidden my bits?

"Do they?" he asks without turning. "I guess we have the same size derriere."

So… with him being taller and bigger than I am, did he just imply that I have a big butt? I mean, I know that I do, but it's not polite for a man to just—

"Can I turn back around now?" The words are dripping with irritation.

"Whatever." I walk over to a section of the locker room that is covered in white tile, but all I find are showers, toilets, and urinals.

"What are you looking for?" he demands.

"A dryer." Even a hand dryer could be helpful, except they have the paper-wasting towel dispensers here.

"If there were a dryer, I would have taken you to it," he grumbles. "I mean, the custodial staff must have one to dry our towels and such, but I have no idea where that is located."

"Oh." I look at him excitedly. "Can we look for it?"

"There is no 'we.' Now that you're not going to freeze to death, you can do whatever the fuck you want."

"Asshole," I mutter under my breath.

Pretending he didn't hear, he strides toward the exit.

Curiosity getting a hold of me once again, I run after him and catch up just in time to see him pulling out an axe from the in-case-of-fire station.

Shit. Have I annoyed him to the point of murder?

But no. Pretending I don't exist, he speed-walks

back to the main entrance and smashes the axe into the door.

Which does nothing. I mean, there's a scratch on the door, but it doesn't yield.

He whacks it again.

Sexy lumberjack vibes galore, but still nothing.

Again.

And again.

"Hey," I say with a wince after he whacks it extra hard. "All you're doing is giving me a headache." And making me far too wet again.

He drops the axe with a loud clang and spins around to face me, his nostrils flaring. "You don't need to be here."

"Oh, really?" I take a step toward him and jut out my chin. "The only reason I'm here is because of the stupid prank you and your team of assholes have pulled."

He narrows his jet-black eyes. "I had nothing to do with the fucking prank."

"Is that so?" I imbue the question with enough sarcasm to kill an extremely sturdy horse. "Did I push *myself* into that pool?"

"I told you that was a fucking misunderstanding."

"Yeah, sure. Whatever." And then I can't resist adding, "*Bearman.*"

The sound that escapes his throat is the closest thing to a growl I've ever heard a human make. For some reason, though, I'm not scared. If anything, I'm even more furious that he doesn't appear inclined to move or actually say anything in response. Like I'm not important, even when I taunt him.

Recklessly, I take another step toward him and give his ridiculously hard chest a shove—which doesn't make him budge one bit, a fact that only infuriates me further. I rise up on my tiptoes and lean in to say right to his face, "Did you hear me? Or have you gone into hibernation?"

His eyes darken further, and another low, furious growl escapes his throat. And I have no idea why this makes me so fucking wet, but it does, and suddenly, instead of shoving him again, I find my hands gripping his face, hard, as I smash my lips against his.

Because I'm so fucking angry. Not for any other reason, I swear.

He must be just as angry because he kisses me back. Fiercely. Punishingly. His arms encircle me in a bear hug, and then we're full-on battling it out with our tongues.

And oh, my god… I may just come.

CHAPTER 4
MICHAEL

Fuuuuuuck.

She is kissing me.

And I'm kissing her back.

Everything fades away. I forget the predicament we're in. I forget how I got here, or where I need to be. This kiss becomes everything, though in some distant periphery of my mind, I'm aware of noises and then of flashes of light.

Fucking fuck. Is it possible to get so hard that you induce a seizure? Is that what the lights in my vision are about?

All I know is that this shouldn't be happening, but it is amazing. She's perfectly soft and tastes like cotton candy. Her delicate feminine scent is maddening and hard to pinpoint—but there are definitely notes of something delicious in there, like roasted cashews dipped in honey.

After a particularly bright flash of light, she pulls away and stares at the doors behind me.

Whatever's got her upset, the rat on her shoulder hisses at it.

I spin around.

The fucking doors are wide open. There are countless people staring at us, including my team and a bunch of firefighters, but my wrath is focused on the paparazzi who are standing there taking pictures.

Of course. Cameras. That's what the flashes were about.

Leaping into action, I reach the closest guy holding a camera, snatch the device out of his hands, and shatter it against the ground.

Seeing this, the rest of the fuckers scatter like cockroaches, and when I try to chase one, Dante and Coach block my way.

"Killing a journalist isn't good PR," Coach warns.

"But I get the therapeutic benefits," Dante adds, more sympathetically.

I glare at the phones in the hands of some of the firefighters. "Everyone took pictures," I growl.

"Probably videos too," Dante says. "What did you expect?"

I expect to break more cameras, and some bones. "Then let me pass." I don't bulldoze through them purely out of respect for Coach.

"Everything is in the cloud," Coach says. "By breaking shit, all you'll do is make the situation worse."

He has a point. "Fucking cloud."

I hate clouds, both the nerd kind in question and the puffs of water vapor in the sky.

"Besides." Dante gestures to the doors. "Aren't you forgetting something? Or someone?"

I turn just in time to see Calliope push her way through the crowd of gawkers.

"Go after her," Dante says.

I frown. "What? Why?"

"I know you haven't had a lot of experience with women," Dante says, "so you may not know this, but women don't like to be abandoned by their boyfriends... especially after coitus. Right, Coach?"

Coach regards me steadily. "My wife wouldn't like that. And that's a fact."

I gape at them. "What the fuck? It's not like that."

Wife? Girlfriend? What's in the water in this town? They know I'm never committing to a woman. It's enough that my parents abandoned me; I'm not giving some random girl that kind of power over me. Unless these two are talking about a casual hookup? I have had those on a rare occasion, but even then, I wouldn't choose someone like her.

Someone who'd want to cuddle after.

Someone I might be tempted to cuddle with... and I hate cuddles.

"Like what?" Dante grins, revealing blindingly white teeth with canines that aren't as pointy as one would expect from someone with such a pale complexion.

I grit my teeth. "It was just a kiss. And a fluke at that."

"Does *she* know that?" Coach asks.

Shit. He's right. I might've given her the wrong idea. I need to correct it, pronto.

Leaving Coach and Dante to gossip like a pair of Catholic schoolgirls, I chase after Calliope—but by the time I get to the parking lot, her little Beetle is already pulling out.

I run out in front of it and slam my hands on the hood. "Fucking wait!"

Shit. She looks like she's contemplating running me over, but then she rolls down her window and sticks out her head. "What?"

I step over to the side of the car. Now that I'm face to face with her, I find myself strangely at a loss for words. "I…" Fuck, what is wrong with me? I force myself to say something, anything. What comes out is, "What the fuck was that?"

"A huge mistake." She punctuates her words by slamming on the gas, and with a screech of tires, her tiny Beetle whooshes out of the parking lot, nearly flattening my toes in the process.

Fucking fuck.

I stand there staring after her until a pale hand lands on my shoulder. "I take it the conversation didn't go so well?" Dante asks when I turn around.

I shake my head.

"Want to get a drink, talk about it?" He gestures at the other side of the parking lot, where the rest of the team are getting on our private charter bus. "Everyone's headed to the pub."

"Fuck no." I hate team-building exercises—almost as much as I hate the overabundant sunshine that blinds everyone, gives them skin cancer, and yet somehow fails to give Dante even a hint of a tan.

"Suit yourself." Dante jogs over to the bus, and they leave.

Good fucking riddance.

Unfortunately, I'm still not out of the woods because Coach is heading my way, no doubt with words of encouragement and wisdom.

"I've got to go!" I yell over to him and beeline for my own car.

CHAPTER 5
CALLIOPE

replay what happened all the way to the circus parking lot. Obviously, the kiss is at the forefront of my mind, particularly how passionate, fierce, and completely and utterly insane it was.

With Wolfgang safely in tow, I slam the car door, hard, and head into the colorful, circular building. What possessed me to do something like that? One second, I wanted to slap the bear with my palm, and then boom, I did so… but with my lips.

Hey. At least it wasn't my pussy. But still… Why that guy, of all people?

Maybe my ex was right. My family and I just might be a little cuckoo in the head.

As if to illustrate my point, when I pass by the kitchen, I spot my dad juggling our toaster, a loaf of bread, and an avocado.

"Hey, Papi," he says as he reaches for the knife—still keeping the rest of the objects in the air as he does. "How was your first day?"

Should I discourage this new attempt at a nickname for me? If we spoke Spanish, it would make more sense for me to call *him* that. Then again, these names *are* getting worse, so maybe I should settle. For all I know, the next one might just be Mini-Me.

"That bad, huh?" he asks, now juggling the knife as well.

Skillfully keeping all the objects circling in the air, he side-eyes my attire, or lack of it, but says nothing. Not that I expected him to. He's probably decided that a jersey and nothing else is what all mascots wear during time off. I'm betting the rest of the family will assume the same.

Skimpy clothes and circus go hand in hand.

"First days are always tough," says Mom's voice from somewhere far down below.

What the hell? Where is she hiding?

I walk around the kitchen counter in search of her—and find her sitting in a deep split, munching on avocado toast. As expected, she doesn't seem the least bit fazed by my attire.

"My day was fine," I lie. "I'm here to get my stuff."

Dad almost drops the toaster. "You're still moving out?"

I nod. "The place they offered me is closer to work." And it's twice the size of my current room, and I don't have to share it with anyone.

"Will you still come home for family dinners?" Mom asks worriedly.

"Of course." I know I'll miss everyone terribly; plus,

I can't cook to save my life, so a home-cooked meal will always be welcome.

"All right," Mom says magnanimously. "Go get ready."

I trek to the room that I share with my oldest sister, and of course, I catch her hanging upside down like a bat, her entire body held up by one foot hooked onto a trapeze that is hanging above the top bunk of our joint bed.

"Hey," she says, her breath unnaturally even considering her position. "How was it?"

"Good."

She narrows her eyes at me. "Just good?"

"Look, Seraphina," I say. "If you want a more in-depth discussion, come down to my eye level. Otherwise, my neck will start to hurt."

As I thought, she clearly isn't that interested because she continues to hang.

I change into normal clothes and walk up to my rat habitat, an object that occupies all the square footage of this room that officially belongs to me.

"Hi, all," I say, pausing Beethoven's "Für Elise," a composition that my little friends greatly enjoy.

Everyone greets me with gleeful chirps and hops. When Wolfgang rejoins the group, their jubilee is through the roof, at least until Marco tries to hump Wolfgang but is then chased away by Polo.

"You teach them anything new lately?" Seraphina asks from her high perch.

I know she's just asking to be polite, but I can't resist pulling out a tiny unicycle and setting Lenin on it.

"Wow," Seraphina says as Lenin makes circles on the table. "He can totally ride that."

Yep. Being the cleverest and the most food-motivated, Lenin is the quickest learner. When I take him from the unicycle and give him his treat, he looks at me thoughtfully:

Tovarisch, I should get a bigger treat for that. It's only fair since I, the rat proletariat, did all the labor here.

"You know, you could resurrect your old act," Seraphina says.

She's talking about the dark days when I rode a unicycle, an activity I enjoyed about as much as a root canal, and the latter is at least done under anesthesia.

"You could hold a circular platform in your hands," my sister continues, "And have the rats ride their unicycles while you ride yours."

I shake my head. "Too dangerous."

She scoffs. "Oh, please. A unicycle act is too dangerous for rats, but walking on a tightrope isn't too dangerous for Grandma?"

I roll my eyes. "You know nobody can stop her." For that matter, is there a way to stop Seraphina herself from leaping to and fro at forty feet in the air?

"Touché," Seraphina says.

"Everyone," I say to the rats, "please don't worry. I'm not taking your toys away. We're just moving." With that, I pack the various tunnels, exercise wheels, social and individual homes, and last but not least, the various toys meant for climbing, chewing, shredding, pushing, carrying, and foraging.

Once everything's all packed into my car, I drive us

over to the new place, where I set up my babies all over again.

"Want to go get the rest of my stuff?" I ask Wolfgang.

He scurries onto my shoulder, and I return to the circus to collect the rest of my possessions—which seem meager in comparison to those of my cute charges.

Once I'm fully settled in my new apartment, I take it in as if for the first time.

The place is spacious and has an amazing lake view, where, just to remind me that we're still in Florida, a giant gator is warming himself on the bank.

"See?" I point at the gator. "That is one of a million reasons why you guys are better off living indoors."

Wolfgang chirps.

Meine Liebe, the main reason to live indoors is not safety. It's because that is where the manna from heaven, also known as cheese, resides.

Lenin grinds his teeth particularly loudly.

If religion is the opium of the humans, cheese is that for the proletari-rat.

"We finally have room for a TV," I tell everyone. Until now, we've been watching movies and shows on the tiny screen of my laptop.

The rats do not seem all that enthused about the prospect of TV, but I sure am.

Now, where will I put it?

I look around and realize that something about the living room is different today compared to the way it was when I first checked it out. There are smudges on the walls, and a few floorboards look like they've been pulled up and then placed back.

How odd. I must have not noticed before.

Whatever. I put on some nice music and get on my laptop to search for the job of my dreams—which obviously isn't dressing up like a hybrid between a clown and a bear. No, what I really want is to produce a live show featuring rats, and I would call it Pied Piper.

For the moment, however, the best I can do is pitch my show to any place that might remotely consider making my dream a reality.

Oh, and I'm realistic enough to know that a show starring rats isn't a traditional form of entertainment. Pied Piper is most likely a pipe dream, especially now that circuses around the US have cut down on animal acts in general. Case in point: the circus where most of my family works asked Grampa to retire his lion show a few years ago.

I smile. Grampa retired along with his show and then used his free time to teach me his craft—all the while thinking that I'd work either with lions like he did, or with bears like his great-grandfather did. When Grampa learned about the rats, he said, and I quote, "The only worse ideas would be working with cockroaches, ticks, or your grandmother."

Regardless, I send out email pitches until my eyes get tired from staring at the screen, and then I head over to my favorite part of this apartment: my very own bedroom.

Damn. There's no bunk bed or snoring trapeze artist on top of it. I look forward to sleeping like a baby who took an Ambien… except that isn't what happens when I actually get into bed.

I'm kept awake by images of dark eyes, strangely sexy scowls, and hair on powerful arms.

Ugh. Is the bear messing with my sleep now?

No. I'm just horny without a specific reason—and now that I have privacy, I can actually do something about it.

I lick my fingers and slide them down under.

"Just make sure you do not think of him," I remind myself as I circle my clit. "Whatever you do, don't think of him."

Yeah, no. The mantra doesn't work, and Michael is exactly what I think about when I come.

But hey. It could have been worse.

I could have screamed his name and scared my rats.

CHAPTER 6
MICHAEL

After I get home and eat, I work on the trickiest part of my secret project: attracting investors. The problem, as usual, is that you have to be cordial when you interface with rich fucks, but cordiality isn't my strong suit. However, being polite is easier in written communication. I just sprinkle in a copious amount of "pleases" and "thank yous." Unfortunately, for the really big investors, face-to-face meetings are unavoidable… and much dreaded by me.

But I'll do whatever it fucking takes.

Once I'm done emailing, I walk over to my telescope and point it at the tallest tree in the forest preserve outside my window.

Whew. The family of hawks is still there, including Eye, the little baby who hatched very recently. Given the local eagles, snakes, owls, and raccoons, I'm always concerned about the chick—which is not something I expected from a hobby like birdwatching.

It was supposed to be fucking relaxing.

Well, it's still relaxing compared to searching for funding, but it used to be more so when it was just the two hawk parents, Ethan and Mo, reinforcing their nest with twigs and leaves. But then Mo laid just one egg, and they took turns carefully incubating said egg for almost a month, guarding the nest and the like, and I got a little invested. Then after I saw them hunt and regurgitate food for young Eye on an hourly basis, I almost got myself a sniper rifle to help them keep predators at bay.

Mo and Ethan deserve to see Eye grow up. Despite their so-called "bird brains," they're much better parents than my human ones were.

My phone rings.

Hmm.

Who could that be?

Turns out, it's Coach—and he's video calling, which he rarely does.

"Hi, Coach," I say, accepting the call.

"Hey," he says. "Just wanted to check on you."

"Why?" Did he not get the fucking clue in the parking lot?

"You got locked inside the arena," he says. "And then there was that kiss with—"

"I'm fine." Or will be, as soon as people stop fucking reminding me about Calliope. "How are you? How are the kids?"

To my surprise, the attempt to deflect actually works, and Coach tells me about his son's latest shenanigans in college, and that his daughter just got promoted to assistant manager. As he talks, I can't help but feel jealous of said kids. Despite being decent people, they seem ungrateful—or at least unaware—of how amazing their father is. He's probably the closest a human male can get to the kind of dad Ethan is.

"Are you sure you're okay?" Coach asks, and I realize I might have missed a few details about his daughter.

"I'm fucking fine, but I do have to go." I don't want to be rude to Coach, but that is what will happen unless he backs the fuck off.

"Sure. See you at practice tomorrow," he says and hangs up.

Right. Fucking practice. I'd better rest for it.

I take my camera and attach it to the telescope to snap a picture of the hawks, then head into the shower to get ready for bed.

While I'm in the shower, I can't help but remember the kiss, and my cock gets painfully hard—so I fist it and fantasize about every porn actress I've ever seen. I definitely don't think about Calliope, with her green eyes, pink hair, and cotton candy taste. Nope, her graceful neck and the way her smooth legs looked in that jersey aren't on my mind at all. Oh, and let's not forget—I mean, I did forget—the fact that she was next to me wearing only a jersey and no panties. Or that—

I grunt as I come, and my mind goes pleasantly blank, which is great because now I'm ready for sleep.

———

I get to the ice rink early in the morning, and Dante is the only one already there, his pale complexion hidden by his goalie gear.

"Hey," I say. "Want to do some drills?"

He takes off his mask, his eyes wide. "You haven't heard, have you?"

I frown. "Heard what?"

"You and the new mascot have gone viral."

CHAPTER 7
CALLIOPE

I wake up because my phone is ringing. Over and over again.

Weird. It's barely dawn. Who could be calling so early, and why?

When I pick up the phone, the first part of my question is answered.

It's Seraphina.

"Hey," I say. "You act so much like a bat already. Are you adopting their schedule now?"

"How could you *not* tell me you kissed a hot hockey player?" she demands. "I saw you last night—as in, *after* it happened."

I gape at the phone. "How could you possibly know that?" Did I talk to myself out loud yet again? And in front of her? I don't recall doing so, but—

"How could anyone *not* know?" she says. "It's all over social media."

Oh. Crap. The cameras from yesterday. But... "Who would care about us kissing?"

"The internet. They've labeled the two of you Honey and Boo Boo."

"What? Why?"

"Something about both of you being bears," she says. "You because you're the mascot, and him because of his personality, and his first and last name."

Huh? What's his name got to do with it?

"At first, it went viral in Russian-speaking countries," she continues. "That's where most of his fans are. But then it started trending with hockey fans in general, and finally, everyone jumped on it. If this keeps up, you two could become as famous as Baby Shark."

"Shit." I walk up to my computer to check out what she's talking about.

"Are you nuts?" she asks. "This is amazing."

"No. I need this job, and this is a surefire way to lose it." Not to mention, I don't want to be forever associated with that mascot outfit—I want to be known for my rat show.

"You could leverage this for your show," Seraphina says, as if reading my thoughts. "I mean… somehow."

"More like, no way."

"Hey, sorry," she says. "Didn't realize I'd be the *bearer* of bad news."

"Was that a bear pun?" I demand.

"That's nothing compared to the comments you'll see online," she says. "After you read them, you'll need a minute to get your *bearings*."

I groan.

"You might also want to choke some of the internet trolls," she says. "With your *bear* hands."

"Seriously?"

"The guy you kissed has a reputation as a bar-*bear*-ian," she says. "Also, they say the two of you are *polar* opposites."

"Stop. Now."

"Why? Is this getting em-*bear*-assing?"

"This isn't funny." I search for "Honey and Boo Boo" and gape at the number of views the video has.

"Bear with me," Seraphina says. "I might get *bear*-y funny after a few more of these."

I hang up right as she says something about *bear*-ly having started, and a bear's right to *bear* arms.

The video I've pulled up is set to the song "Bi-Polar Bear" by Stone Temple Pilots. It shows our kiss, but it's also interspersed with a bunch of other videos. Most of them are of Michael punching someone's face on the ice or scoring a goal, but there's also the video of me from a few weeks ago, capturing the time I got caught with Wolfgang hiding under my theme park outfit.

Fuck me. Until today, only theme parks had black-listed me over the "rat incident," but now the whole world knows about it. If I lose my current gig—which seems likely—I won't be able to get a job in any industry where they don't like rats, which is most of them.

Oh, and I can't help but make the mistake of reading the comments.

At the top, there are all the bear jokes, most of which make Seraphina's puns seem like first-born cubs in comparison. But below that are mean personal attacks. The worst insinuate that I'm a slut and pick apart my looks, while the mildest ones make fun of our names. They call *me* "Clown Butt Bear" on account of my last name and my mascot outfit. Michael is labeled "Grouchy Bear" because his last name means "Of Bear" in Russian, and his first name shortens to "Misha," which is also bear-related.

Is that why he is so touchy about bear comparisons?

Must be. It might also explain why he hates the mascot so much, along with the name of his—I mean our—team. If I ended up on a team called the Clown Butts, and it had a mascot that looked like a giant clown's ass, I wouldn't be a happy camper either. If I had a penny for every time I was teased with "clown butt" jokes over the years, I'd be able to afford an army of clowns by now, an army that I would order to locate the fuckers who teased me and stuff balloon animals up their asses.

Oh, and more than a few people are theorizing as to why Wolfgang is on my shoulder, with too many bestiality theories even for the internet.

But hey, not all the comments are nasty. A bunch of people are simply rooting for Honey and Boo Boo to get married and have lots of furry cubs.

Yeah, no. After my last breakup, I'm not interested in dating, let alone marriage. What's the point of meeting someone and going on dates when they'll break up with you as soon as they meet your family? And marriage? Forget it. No sane man would willingly become a part of the Klaunbut clan. My only option might just be to marry a distant Klaunbut cousin, of which I have countless. Needless to say, if I don't go the cousin route, the last non-Klaunbut I'd consider would be Mr. Grouchy Bear.

Especially if by some miracle I keep my current job. My ex was a coworker, and I had to switch parks after we broke up, so I'm not repeating *that* mistake again.

Having said all that, looking at us kissing is making my insides feel gooey.

Stupid insides.

It's probably just hunger. Or thirst. Real thirst, I mean, not a euphemism.

I look at myself in the mirror. "Maybe I should make a large fruit salad to take care of both those needs?"

Then I reply, "Sure, but just in case, don't use a banana."

Meal prepped, I share some fruit with my rats, and then I eat the rest.

Hmm. Even thus fortified, I do not become immune to watching that kiss over and over again.

Ugh. I need to stop this.

It's time to go to work anyway.

I take Wolfgang and get into my car for the short drive to my workplace. I'm not sure what I expect when I get there, but as soon as I'm parked, I'm accosted by Coach, the HR woman I spoke to, and two of the players from yesterday.

"Hello," I say as my heart drops. "To what do I owe this welcome greeting?"

But of course, I already know what they'll say. They're here to inform me that I'm fired, and the two players will serve as security in case I try to fight my way in.

Given that everyone knows about Wolfgang anyway, I make his day by letting him perch on my shoulder instead of hiding in my pocket or purse as I usually would until I got myself into my outfit.

"We figured you'd want some help getting into the building," Coach says, seemingly unperturbed by the rat on my shoulder.

I blink at him. "You want me *in* the building?" Is that where the firing conversation is to take place?

"Well, yeah," he says. "You officially start today, don't you?"

"Right." I'm about to set some sort of record when it comes to getting fired.

"Come then. Sorry about the circus."

Circus? Is my family here?

No. It's worse. A mob of journalists is milling by the entrance to the building, and judging by all the cameras pointed at me, this might have something to do with that viral video.

"Get the fuck out of our way," says one of the players, pushing aside a dozen of the newspeople at once.

Ah. The players have taken on the roles of bouncers, but *for* me, not against me.

Interesting.

Once we're finally inside, the HR woman—who reminds me that her name is Linda—asks for me and Coach to follow her into the conference room near her office.

So I *am* getting fired?

"Is Michael in there already?" Coach asks.

Why would he need to be at my firing?

"He's in there," Linda says. "So is Adam from PR and Eve from Finance."

PR? Finance? Curiouser and curiouser. Maybe they're going to ask me not to badmouth them after I'm fired, and to that end, they plan to pay me a generous severance?

I wouldn't mind that at all.

When we enter the conference room, Adam and Eve are already waiting—dressed in business suits, not fig leaves. Also waiting is Michael, and seeing him again is like a kick in the ovaries. He has a muscle shirt on, with delectable chest hair peeking out, and sports a five-o'clock shadow—which everyone knows is the sexiest kind of shadow. Oh, and for some reason, he's glaring at the players who escorted us in.

"You can go," Coach says to said players.

The two look all too happy to leave, no doubt because they've also noticed Michael's black-as-his-soul eyes beaming death rays their way.

Not a single person seems to care that Wolfgang is sitting on my shoulder, which makes me like them all, with the exception of the bear, of course, who probably just doesn't look at me enough to notice anything at all.

"Want to sit there?" Coach points at the chair next to Michael.

I narrow my eyes. "Why would I want to sit next to *him*?"

Coach shrugs. "What we have to say concerns the two of you, so it will just make life a little easier." He gestures at a chair across from Michael. "You can sit there if you'd prefer."

"No. It's fine." I plop into the chair next to Michael and immediately curse my choice. Just like yesterday, he smells mouthwateringly good: like herbs, mushrooms, and honey.

"What the fuck is all this about?" Michael growls as soon as everyone is seated.

"I might not have put it in those exact terms, but yeah," I say. "Why are we here?"

Eve clears her throat. "I got a call from my equivalent with the Yetis. The tickets to the exhibition game are sold out."

Everyone except me stares at her with different levels of shocked expressions.

Adam scratches the back of his head. "The same game that was going to get canceled because the Yetis couldn't sell any tickets?"

Eve nods triumphantly.

"Who or what are the Yetis?" I ask no one in particular.

On my shoulder, Wolfgang cleans his whiskers.

Meine Liebe, a yeti is another word for bigfoot, and bigfoot sounds like a creature that smells strongly like feet, which—given that feet smell like cheese—tells me that whatever or whoever the Yetis are, they smell delicious.

"The Yetis are a New York hockey team," Coach says. "Michael was with them for a short while, and he recently used that connection to set up an outside-league game with them, a big deal because they're much stronger and—"

"They're not that much stronger," Michael growls. "We just—"

"Gentlemen," Eve says pointedly. "I wasn't finished."

Everyone stops talking and looks at Eve, even Wolfgang.

"As I was saying," Eve continues. "All of our other games have sold out as well, even the one against the Pineapple Ice Surfers."

Once again, everyone's jaws drop, and again, Wolfgang and I are the exceptions.

"Who are the Pineapple Ice Surfers?" I ask.

"The Hawaiian team," Michael says. "They are the worst in the DHL, and no one ever comes to see them get slaughtered live. Not unless the game takes place *in* Hawaii."

"And that's not the case this time," Coach says. "They're coming here for that one."

"That's correct," Eve says. "The financial implications are huge." She looks meaningfully at Adam. "I presume things are equally bright on your end?"

He nods. "Fortunately, Michael breaking that camera didn't make the news," he says. "Neither did the team demolishing the bar yesterday. Or—"

"Why the fuck are *we* here?" Michael gestures at me. "Can someone get around to explaining that?"

Coach, Adam, and Eve all look meaningfully at Linda.

"Why do I have to explain it?" Linda demands.

"Because it's delicate?" Coach says, a bit tentatively.

"And you're in HR," Adam adds.

"Fine." Linda faces us. "This meeting is to discuss the impact of Honey and Boo Boo."

Oh.

"What the fuck is Honey and Boo Boo?" Michael demands.

"Us," I say, cringing. "Though I'm not sure which of us is which."

Michael grunts in frustration. "That viral fucking video."

"No, it's a kissing video," Adam says. "But if you think another video with some *other* activity might surface, it would make my job easier if you tell me now."

"What other video could there be?" I ask, but what I really mean is, "How slutty does Adam think I am?"

"I thought we'd established that I'd handle the talking?" Linda says icily to Adam, and you can tell she wants to smack him but restrains herself due to HR policy.

"Please," Adam says sheepishly. "Go on."

"Thank you," Linda says. "As I started to say, the video is having a very positive impact on this team, and given the financial troubles we've been facing"—she gestures at Eve—"this development couldn't have come at a better time."

Everyone except me, Michael, and Wolfgang nods.

"You're welcome," I say tentatively.

"And get to the fucking point," Michael growls.

Linda sighs. "Right. The point." She puts her hands in a praying position and touches her nose. "With your cooperation, we'd like to keep the public interest going."

"And are willing to compensate you," Eve chimes

in. "For the inconvenience that said cooperation might cause."

"Huh?" I glance at Michael to check if he's following this.

He isn't, or so I figure because he puts the question a lot more eloquently than I would when he shouts, "What the fuck do you fucks need us to fucking do?"

"Nothing bad," Linda says a bit too quickly. "Just a little PR stunt, is all." She turns to Adam. "Do you want to jump in?"

Adam glances worriedly at Michael. "I thought you wanted to do the talking."

"For God's sake," Eve says. "First things first: are the two of you dating?"

"Fuck no," Michael says and shakes his head so vehemently the resulting gust of wind nearly blows Wolfgang off my shoulder.

Hey. Does he need to act like us dating is so unthinkable?

"I just joined the team," I say. "When would we have had the time to date?"

Eve shrugs. "You could've met prior, but yes, we didn't think it was likely. I just had to check." She looks pointedly at Linda. "Do you want me to say it, or will you?"

"Could you?" Linda looks ready to climb under the table.

Eve sighs. "We want you to keep up the charade."

"What?" Michael and I ask in unison.

"Everyone thinks you're a couple," Eve says. "Or

wants to believe that you are. So, to that end, it would be great if you *were* dating. Pretending to date, that is."

Oh, no. No. No. No. I can't believe I didn't see where this was going, but now—

Michael leaps to his feet. "I'm going to fucking *pretend* you didn't just fucking say that."

Seriously, why is he acting like I'm a leper?

"Michael, please," Coach says soothingly. "The team needs this."

Looking sullen, Michael sits back down. "This is fucking insane."

"Well," Eve says. "We realize this is an unconventional request, hence the extra compensation." She clears her throat and looks pointedly at Linda.

"And HR gives our full blessing, of course." Linda fiddles with a folder in front of her. "We do not have a rule that forbids a mascot from dating a player, so—"

"Unconventional?" I exclaim. "Unconventional would be asking me to unicycle to work in my mascot outfit. Or asking Michael here to be polite for ten minutes straight. What you're asking is—"

"A big favor," Eve butts in. "For which we're willing to put an extra zero at the end of your salary."

I don't know how I sense this, but at the mention of that much money, Michael tenses next to me. "Do both of us get that bump?" he demands.

"Correct," Coach says meaningfully. "And you'll get a bonus upfront, as a sign of our goodwill."

"How much?" I ask, unable to believe I'm even considering this.

Eve writes something on two business cards, then hands one to me and the other to Michael.

When I see my amount, I almost drop the paper. For this much, I'd pretend to date an actual bear, and maybe consider letting him get to second base.

"You get to keep the bonus if you keep up the pretense until the Yetis game," Linda elaborates. "And the salary bump continues for as long as the good PR from the 'relationship' does."

"Fucking fuck," Michael says, his eyes on his paper. "We'll do it."

"Ex-fucking-cuse me?" I whirl on him. "We will not do anything until both of us agree."

His jaw twitches. "My apologies, *ptichka*. Will you or will you not participate in this fucking charade?"

I narrow my eyes. "What's a *ptichka*?"

"Translated from Russian, it means 'little bird,'" he says. "I figure if we're dating, we'll need pet names for each other—and the day I call anyone Honey or Boo Boo is the day I shoot myself in the fucking head."

Hmm. Little Bird is better than either Honey or Boo Boo, but I'm not going to tell him that. "Fine, *Pooh*, I will participate in the charade."

His eyes become tiny coals. "Pooh, as in *Winnie the*?"

"Ah, right." I bat my eyelashes at him innocently. "Sorry, Shmoopy, I forgot how sensitive you are when it comes to… teddies."

Michael balls his hands. "This will never fucking work."

"It has to," Eve says. "I'm sure she can call you something other than Shmoopy."

"And since we're on that subject," Adam says. "Are we sure Honey and Boo Boo can't be an option?"

Michael slams his fist on the table. "Mention those names again, and I'm out."

"How about *tsar*?" Linda asks. "That's Russian, like *ptichka*."

"Doesn't it mean 'king?'" I demand.

"Emperor." A smug smile touches the corners of Michael's lips, and it makes me remember how it felt when I was kissing them.

"No way," I say, both to my treacherous memory and the *tsar* suggestion. "Also, before anyone asks, also out of the question are words like sir, master, and daddy."

"How about bunny?" Linda asks. "What does that sound like in Russian?"

"As in 'Honey Bunny?'" Eve clarifies.

"No fucking honey." Michael practically roars the sentence, like a honey-deprived bear.

"Can I steer clear of Russian altogether?" I suggest. "I don't speak it, so it would be suspicious if—"

"Fucking fine," Michael growls. "Call me boo."

"Boo Boo?" Adam asks in a loud whisper.

"No," Michael replies menacingly. "A singular fucking boo."

"Calm down, boo," I say. "Adam's just thinking about the PR of the whole thing, not trying to hurt your fuzzy feelings."

Adam looks at me gratefully, and I can tell he wants to continue the double Boo/Honey debate, but is afraid to.

Michael takes in a deep breath, then blows it out with an annoyed whoosh. His voice is a touch less growly as he says, "I think we've gotten sidetracked with the nicknames, and I take responsibility for that. What we really should discuss is, how are we supposed to make people believe that we're a couple?"

I whip around to face him, my hand ready to slap his cheek. "Are you saying I don't look like someone you would date?"

"No." Michael looks at the ceiling as if he's hoping a lightning strike will put him out of his misery. "What I meant was... I haven't dated in years. Everyone knows this."

Why do I like that factoid? Is something wrong with me?

Adam perks up. "Your lack of dating is why the video caught the initial attention of your fans. As to how to make people believe—don't worry about that. In fact, your official statements can be that you're 'just friends.' What you need to do is be seen together as much as possible, 'accidentally' allow paparazzi to take more photos, and strategically stage another kiss."

Before I can violently protest, Linda clears her throat. "You don't need to kiss, or partake in any intimacy for that matter."

"Right, right," Adam says, looking majorly disappointed. "Just spend time together, and when it comes to touching and whatnot, do as much as you're comfortable with."

"Or none at all," Linda says insistently.

At the thought of Michael touching me "and whatnot," a blush spreads from my toes to the very top of my head. "Where do you suggest we go to be seen?"

Adam shrugs. "Visit sick kids? Be there for Michael after his games?"

"I'm a mascot on the team," I say. "I'll be there for the games regardless."

Adam's eyes light up. "Right. Sorry. But here's another idea: when you're dressed as the mascot, mess with Michael more than you would mess with the rest of the team."

I like this last suggestion, especially because it makes Michael produce a sound like he's been caught in a bear trap.

Coach shifts in his seat. "I have an idea of my own."

We all look at the man as he faces Michael. "You should tell some of your gossipier teammates that you're dating, and that she's off-limits."

"I already did that," Michael snaps. "I mean, the off-limits bit. I told Jack and said to tell the others—not that it fucking helped."

He told them I was off-limits? The nerve of this guy.

But also, it feels kind of nice to know.

"Good," Coach says. "Now just add the bit about you two dating—and mention that it's a secret from HR or something like that. That will almost guarantee they'll gossip about it."

You'd think he were talking about a knitting circle and not a bunch of macho dudes.

Suddenly, a panting woman runs into the conference room, her lipstick smeared and hair disheveled, like she just got properly fucked a few minutes ago. "I'm sorry I'm late," she says. "Did I miss anything?"

"They've just agreed," Coach says. "And we're about to adjourn. Practice is about to—"

"That is so great." She looks my way. "Hi, I'm Amelia, the general manager for the team. Sorry again. I was in a meeting with Mr. Ironside, the owner." Her eyes suddenly widen. "Is that *the* rat?"

I half expect her to jump on the table and squeal—a surprisingly common reaction from the female of our species—but she actually runs toward Wolfgang and grins like a loon. "She's so much cuter in person than she is on the video."

"He's a male," I say, unable to help an answering grin.

"Ah," she says. "My apologies. Of course. Now that you mention it, I realize how very handsome *he* is."

Wolfgang puffs up.

Meine Liebe, give this human some cheese—such good behavior must be rewarded.

"What kind of a rat is he?" Amelia carefully touches the top of Wolfgang's head, and he generously lets her keep her finger.

"He's a dumbo rat," I say. "Hence the round ears, large head, small jaw, and wide eyes."

"What's his name?" Amelia asks. "Wait, let me guess: Remy?"

I grin wider. "That *is* my favorite fictional character of all time, but naming one of my *dumbo* rats something like that would be asking for a cease-and-desist letter from Disney. But you're close. His name is Wolfgang, after Wolfgang Puck, another famous chef."

"Puck, huh? That's a link to hockey." She looks approvingly at Linda and Coach. "You guys should have told me you've gotten us two mascots for the price of one."

Interesting. "You know," I say nonchalantly. "I could put Wolfgang on my shoulder while I'm inside Mr. Bloom." Wait, did that sound like I'm planning to fuck the mascot?

"I love that idea." Amelia looks authoritatively around the room. "Please do what is needed to make that happen."

Linda looks at Wolfgang as if for the first time. "There could be some concerns from—"

"We can just say he's her emotional support animal," Eve interjects. "That's what I did for Lucie, my pet monitor lizard."

Wolfgang looks at me worriedly.

Meine Liebe… why does that last word make me feel like I've suddenly become a delectable slice of cheese?

Adam pales. "You don't happen to have Lucie with you, by any chance?"

"What? No," Eve says with a narrowed gaze. "Lucie is a big girl, so in what orifice do you imagine I might be hiding her?"

"Please do *not* answer that," Linda says in a panicked voice. More calmly, she adds, "I think I speak for everyone when I deem this meeting successfully concluded."

CHAPTER 8
MICHAEL

oncluded? What the fuck? What about the logistics? If I'm supposedly dating Calliope, there's—

Everyone leaps to their feet, and the room empties faster than you can spell "cowards." The only one who isn't running is Calliope, but I suspect that has more to do with the rat on her shoulder than any bravery.

"We should talk," I tell her grudgingly.

She turns my way, a perfectly shaped eyebrow raised. "Oh? Why?"

I sigh. "How are we going to pull this off?"

"Ah. That." She runs her hand through her hair, her nails as sparkly as the rest of her. "Who cares about the pesky details, right?" She makes air quotes. "The meeting was 'successfully concluded.'"

I shrug. "Linda probably wanted us to discuss the minutia amongst ourselves, like adults."

"Like adults? What is that supposed to mean?"

Fuck me. "Are your feathers always so easy to ruffle?"

She gapes at me. "People who live in glass houses shouldn't throw pucks."

I grit my teeth and strive for what little patience I possess. "I get it. You need to process all of this. Maybe we can talk after practice?"

"And maybe you should bite me." She turns on her heel and strides out of the conference room.

"That may not be a bad idea," I say without thinking —though, in my defense, this is the first time I've borne witness to the marvel that is her rear end. I mean, butts have always been my weakness, especially ones with plenty to grab during doggy style, but *ptichka's* ass is on another level. If there were a competition for the juiciest derrière, she'd win it without even needing to bend. And if she did bend—

She slams the conference door almost in my face.

I leave the room and follow her in silence, my dick painfully hard on account of the view. When we get to the locker room, I frown, and when she tries to go inside, I grab her shoulder—a firm, shapely shoulder, to be exact.

"What the hell are you doing?" she demands, eyes on my hand as if it were a cobra.

"Right back at you." I remove my hand. "Practice is about to start. There are naked assholes in there."

"Oh." She shuffles from foot to foot. "I forgot my costume inside."

"Right. I know. It was there when I came in this

morning. I hid it in my locker for you." And sure, maybe I took a whiff of the disembodied bear's head to check if *ptichka* truly smells like cotton candy, and she does, but that was just a momentary lapse of reason. "You also forgot your other clothes." Including her panties, which I didn't sniff, no matter how tempting the proposition. "I've got it all stashed away."

"You do?" She looks at me and then at her rat, as if she wants him to confirm she heard me correctly.

"It's no big deal," I reply gruffly. "If I hadn't, those assholes in there could have messed with your stuff." And then I would have had to break some bones, which would've meant we'd be a player short while flying to New York to play the Yetis.

"Thanks." She bats her eyelashes prettily. "Can you bring those to my changing room?"

"Sure." I head into the locker room—and am met with hoots and cheers.

"What the fuck?" I demand from all the leering faces.

"The video," Isaac says for everyone in a rare feat of leadership. "You're famous."

Fuck. I guess this is a segue. "It's good you all saw that. Saves me the time to explain what will happen to the balls of anyone who so much as looks at Calliope the wrong way."

Jack pales so much his skin is almost as alabaster as Dante's. "I've already told them she's off limits."

"That was yesterday," I growl. "As of now, she's more than off limits. She's mine." I meet the gaze of each player one by one, so there can be no mistake that

I'm being heard. "Anyone who comes near her will become a eunuch."

There. Not as subtle as Coach would have suggested, but they know all they need to know and are free to gossip... unless I've scared them out of doing even that. Or unless they respect the unwritten rule that states "what happens in the locker room stays in the locker room." All I know is, there's no sign of cheering or snickering when I grab the mascot costume from my locker, and the silence continues even when I pull out Calliope's clothes... including her panties.

Good. The fuckers must be smarter than I've given them credit for.

Leaving the locker room, I stride over to the closet that's become Calliope's changing room and find the door wide open. She's inside, scanning her surroundings in dismay.

"What's wrong?" I growl.

"Like you don't know?" She glares at me. "Do you and the rest of the brutes think it's funny to ransack my room like this?"

Fuck. She's right. It looks as though someone went through all the shit in this room and then didn't put it back the way it ought to be afterward.

"Whoever did this wasn't anyone on the team," I say coldly.

They're not suicidal.

"Who then?" she demands.

Great fucking question. "I don't know, but we can start by talking to security."

"Oh." She brightens. "You think there's a camera monitoring the door?"

"Better fucking be."

Together, we head over to the security office, where we learn that no, there are no cameras by the door to her changing room or in any of the hallways near it.

"As of today, there will be," I tell the guy.

"What do you mean?" he asks. "The budget—"

I toss a few hundred dollars at him. "I don't care if you have to go to RadioShack yourself. Get it done. I'll be back to check."

"RadioShack?" Calliope says as we're headed back. "Is he supposed to jump into a time machine and go back to 2014?"

I frown. "This isn't a joking matter. Someone broke into your changing room." And when I find out who, there will be hell to pay.

"Could it be related to the stuff online?" she asks. "Maybe I've gained an overeager fan?"

I halt in my tracks. "You mean a stalker?"

"Well, I guess I do. My youngest sister is a… performer, and she had one once. He was pretty harmless, and after one of my brothers had a talk with him, he left her alone."

Sure, her brother "talked" with the stalker. I'm sure no hammers or pliers were involved. "Stalkers aren't harmless," I say firmly. "If there is one, I'm going to find him and make sure this doesn't happen again."

If growing up in an orphanage in Russia has taught me anything, it's how to properly deal with people who cross me.

"It's probably not a stalker," she says. "I still think it's more likely a prank by your teammates."

Hmm. "I'll ask them about it now," I tell her. "See you on the rink." I turn to leave, but this time she's the one who puts a hand on my shoulder, and the feeling of her delicate fingers makes me instantly hard.

"What?" I demand without turning.

"How do I get to the rink?"

Oh. I tell her, then get back to the locker room just in time to catch my teammates gearing up.

"Did anyone go into her dressing room?" I demand. "Admit it now, and I might be merciful." By which I mean I'll only break half the bones I would have otherwise.

They take turns reminding me that Jack told them she was off limits, and therefore they obviously wouldn't go anywhere near her room.

"Then she might have a stalker," I say grimly. "If you see anything sketchy, let me know immediately."

"We will," Isaac says solemnly.

"Yeah," everyone echoes.

With that, they finish gearing up and leave, and I follow close behind them.

Once we're on the ice, I channel my frustration into the practice, and it must be a success because Coach calls me over and tells me that if I keep this up, we might actually beat the Yetis in New York.

Hearing a couple of muffled giggles, I realize that everyone has paused to watch Calliope riding a unicycle on the ice with her rat on her shoulder and what seems to be a pie in her hands—or at least I assume it's Calliope. She has the mascot head on.

How is she keeping her balance? And in that suit? Remarkable.

"Boo!" she screams, making her voice deeper. "Are you done with practice?"

Now the giggles turn into chuckles, and everyone looks at me.

"Oh, yes," Dante replies to her. "Boo was a beast today, but he is done and is all yours."

She rides the unicycle over, then parks it near us, and wobbles over the remaining distance.

"Boo," she says eagerly.

"Ptichka," I say with a lot more reservation. "If you're thinking of—"

Bam.

The pie slams into my face, as I strongly suspected it might.

A hushed silence descends on the rink, and Coach puts a calming hand on my shoulder, all of which I find extremely insulting.

Even if she were about to murder me, I wouldn't hurt a woman. Especially *this* woman.

Taking a finger, I scrape some cream off my face and put the finger in my mouth.

"Thank you," I say loudly. "Next time, please make it cotton candy-flavored."

Like a bubble bursting, everyone laughs uproariously and, in my opinion, disproportionately to how funny the situation is.

Dante skates over and takes off his goalie mask. "Boo, it seems like you can skip your daily facial."

Calliope chuckles.

"Go to the dick, Nosferatu." I wipe all remnants of cream off my face with my sleeve.

Calliope salutes Coach. "Mr. Bloom reporting for duty, Coach," she says as though she didn't just assault me with a confectionary. "Anything I should practice today?"

The corners of Coach's eyes crinkle. "Your job is pretty free flowing. The only thing you *have* to do is learn how to give an autograph as Mr. Bloom so it matches the way Ted and his predecessors did it. Otherwise, you can use your own creativity if you wish. That is, unless you want my help?"

"I'm good," she says. "I've watched some videos of the shenanigans Ted used to pull, and I think I can improve upon them." She gestures at the unicycle with her fluffy paw. "One question I had was: do you need me to skate, or can I walk when I'm not on my unicycle? I know how to rollerblade, but—"

"That can help, sure," Coach says. "You need balance for both, but given your unicycle skills, I'm sure you have that aplenty. Forward movement is similar. Turns are easier on the ice. Stopping is the thing that's going to be quite different."

"So I'll work on stopping," she says. "Though for now, given this suit, I can just crash into something or someone when I need to stop."

If it's *someone*, they had better be me.

"Is there any chance you have skates in my size?" Calliope asks. "I'm suddenly dying to try them."

Coach surreptitiously looks at me, and I give him an imperceptible nod—mostly because I'm curious how quickly she will learn to ice skate.

"What size shoe do you wear?" Coach asks.

"Nine," she says.

"That's a child's seven and a half, right?" Coach asks.

She cocks her giant clown-bear head. "How would I know that?"

"Sorry," Coach says. "Once you have kids, you do that sort of conversion all the time." He turns my way. "Michael, do you happen to know where we can get ice skates in that size?"

He knows that I do, so instead of replying, I march away to locate a few pairs of skates that are around that size—though a part of me wishes I'd measured Calliope's foot first, since that is the way skate fitting is supposed to be done.

Yeah. It's not like I want to see and touch her feet. Or check if she's got sparkly nail polish on her toes to match her fingers. Or if she wears a toe ring. Or an ankle bracelet. No. You just have to be measured to get properly fitting skates, that is all.

When I return, Calliope has her mascot head off, and when I hand her the first pair of skates to try on, she narrows her eyes at me. "Why do you have these on hand?" She scans my teammates. "I doubt any of your fellow Neanderthals wear dainty skates like these."

I take a deep sigh. "A thank you might be a more

appropriate response." There's no way I'm discussing my secret project right now.

She waltzes over and leans in to whisper into my ear. "Do you use these to seduce puck bunnies?"

Her lips brush my ear, and I thank the hockey gods for my protective cup. Otherwise, she'd be able to see my raging erection, and so would everyone else.

"Why?" I whisper back. "Are you jealous?"

She huffs indignantly. "If we're pretending to date, we have to also at least pretend not to be with anyone else."

My jaw ticks. "That's absolutely correct, *ptichka*. I will not even look at anyone else, and no man but me is to come within six feet of you."

Muttering "bar-bear-ian" under her breath, she nevertheless nods and then tries on the various pairs of skates before settling on a pink pair with glitter-like sparkles sewn on—of course.

As soon as she hits the ice, she's able to move gracefully, or as gracefully as is possible for a giant plush bear. When I spot my teammates watching her with too much curiosity, I suggest to Coach to call the practice over and hint that he might find himself a few players short otherwise.

Coach uses his whistle and sends the assholes to the locker room.

Meanwhile, Calliope is skating better and better, though as soon as I get on the ice, she slams into me—which could be a prank but is more likely the only way she knows how to stop.

"I have to go now," Coach says. "Michael, can you do me a favor and teach Calliope how to stop?"

Calliope pushes away from me. "I don't need his help."

Coach grins. "You two make a cute couple."

With that, he leaves, and if he had been anyone but Coach, I'd tell him wholeheartedly to go to the fucking dick.

CHAPTER 9
CALLIOPE

gnoring my assurances that his help isn't needed—
or wanted—Michael explains to me something
called a snow plow stop.

I set Wolfgang on a nearby bench and attempt the
maneuver. It turns out to be pretty easy. Next, Michael
teaches me another way to stop, where I have to drag
the skate back and angle it, which is a little trickier, but I
make it work.

"You're a quick learner," he says approvingly once I
master the fourth technique he shows me.

"And you're a condescending jerk," I reply. "Just
teach me the best way to do this, and let's get the hell
out of here."

Arching an eyebrow, he skates away, picks up speed,
and then stops so suddenly I can scarcely believe my
eyes. "You mean, like this?"

Shit. "Yeah. Sure. Anything you can do I can do
better."

Great. I sound like that musical where someone gets her gun—which is trivial here in Florida.

"Okay," he says skeptically. "Turn your skates in a perpendicular direction from where you're headed and use the edges of the blades to create friction. It's called a hockey stop."

Is he saying words like "friction" to turn me on? Because it's not working. I'm not tempted to slip my arm out of my costume's sleeve to touch myself—all under the cover of layers of fake bear-fur. Nope. Not tempted at all.

"—got all that?" he demands.

Shit. I might have spaced out there for a second. "Show it to me again."

He does, and I realize I must have some sort of skating fetish—or competency fetish—because I never would have expected that seeing someone come to a sudden halt on ice would make me this hot and bothered.

"Like this?" I speed up and try his method—and promptly fall, the suit assuring that only my pride is hurt in the process.

He skates over and lifts me up with a gentleness I didn't think him capable of. "Are you okay?"

"Yeah. Fine." I try to pull away. "Just need to practice that a few more times."

"No," he says imperiously, not letting go. "Let's make sure you're not hurt." He lifts me up like a sack of teddy bears and carries me somewhere as I protest loudly.

When a janitor spots us, he winks at Michael knowingly, which pisses me off almost as much as the manhandling does.

Finally, he puts me down next to a door labeled "MEDICAL."

Inside, a woman tells me that she's an orthopedic surgeon, and per Michael's demands, she insists I get out of the suit so I can be checked.

"No." I stomp my fuzzy foot to punctuate the word. "I have to go get Wolfgang."

"I'll get him," Michael says and leaves before I can raise any sort of objection.

"That's just great," I tell the doctor. "You're about to have two patients." Because Wolfgang will surely bite the asshole. I'm the only human he trusts to pick him up.

"Is Wolfgang a dog?" the doctor asks.

"No." I don't clarify that he's a rat in case the good doctor is one of those jumps-on-furniture-when-frightened females. There aren't many places of elevation in this tiny room.

"Can you take that thing off?" She pokes at my costumed bicep with a smirk.

I do so, grateful that I'm wearing my short shorts and a tank top underneath instead of just my bra and panties.

She quickly examines me and tells me that I'm totally fine.

"I know," I say. "It was Michael who—"

Speak of the devil. He waltzes in, and a surprisingly content-looking Wolfgang is perched on his shoulder.

Hell, the little traitor even chirps excitedly, like he's scored a slice of cheese.

Well, at least Wolfgang jumps over to my shoulder as soon as Michael is within leaping distance. Otherwise, I don't know what I would have done.

"Oh," the doctor says. "Wolfgang is your rat. I should have guessed."

"What do you mean?" I ask. "How often do you assume people have rats?"

"Honey, everyone saw the YouTube video," she says.

"I call her *ptichka*," Michael growls. "*Not* honey."

The doctor looks nonplussed. "That's good for you…"

"Is she hurt?" Michael demands.

"Boo, I'm perfectly fine," I say in a saccharine voice.

The doctor nods, and Michael looks so relieved that it tugs on something in my chest.

Wait. What? I'm being silly. The brute was just worried because I never signed any sort of a liability waiver before his lesson. He couldn't care less about me, I'm sure of that.

"Is that what you plan wear under that outfit every day?" Michael asks, his black eyes glinting dangerously for some unknown reason.

"Sometimes," I say. "Sometimes even less."

"Less?" His nostrils flare.

"What business is it of yours?" I demand, and then recall we're supposed to be dating.

"Fucking fuck," he growls and rushes out of the little office, slamming the door on his way out.

"All hockey players are hotheads," the doctor says sagely. "I'm sure he'll cool off and apologize for that later."

Does that mean she still thinks we're together? "Thanks, doctor," I say as I pick up my suit.

"You're not putting it back on?" she asks.

"Why?"

She shrugs. "Some guy might whistle at you, and Michael might overhear and—"

"That's ridiculous." But I yank on the suit. "Happy now?"

"I had nothing to do with this," the doctor says. "Please take care."

Holding my head high, I leave the office and return to the ice.

To my relief, no overbearing assholes are around, so I focus on mastering stopping the way Michael showed me. Just as the Zamboni machine shows up to spruce up the ice, I nail a perfect stop, but my excitement is cut short by a slow clapping behind me.

I execute a figure-skating-like spin to see who's there.

Surprise, surprise, it's Michael. I mean, who else would be here to rain on my parade?

"You spying on me?" I skate over to where he is standing and stop perfectly once again.

He shrugs. "Someone has to make sure you don't break something."

"I'm perfectly fine without you," I say, and, of course, nearly fall on my ass for no reason at all.

"That should be a clue that you've overtrained," he growls. "Can you finally go change?"

I set my jaw. "Why do you care?"

He sighs. "I'm starving."

"So go eat," I snap. "What does that have to do with me?"

Unless it is me that he wants to eat. It's eerily easy to picture those masculine lips on my—

Said lips vibrate as he blows out a frustrated breath. "Coach asked that I walk you to your car. The vultures are still outside."

Oh. I forgot.

"Does Coach want them to see us together?" I ask. "Or is he actually worried about my safety?"

"For fuck's sake, does it matter?" Michael points at the exit. "Can we go?" His stomach growls, loudly.

"Fine."

I only remember my great-grandfather vaguely, but I'm pretty sure one of the pearls of wisdom that he passed on to me was, "There's nothing more dangerous than a hungry bear."

As Michael stalks me to my changing room, I make a point not to speak, and he doesn't break the silence.

Once inside, I take off the mascot suit and debate if I should stay in the skimpy clothing, just to piss him off.

But no. I don't want to leave my day clothes here for the hypothetical stalker to mess with, and if I carry them with me, my ploy will be transparent.

So I change, and when I exit, I catch him scanning me from head to toe again, and nodding approvingly— which pisses me off.

I walk up to him and poke his chest with my finger —a mistake because touching his hair there does things to me. Inappropriate things. "Let's get something straight. I wear whatever I want."

"Sure, *ptichka*. Who said you couldn't?"

Is this a joke? "You did. Or implied it."

His eyes heat up. "You can walk around naked if you so wish. I'll just deal with every asshole who dares to ogle you."

Is "deal with" a euphemism for "break the neck of"?

"Why do I even bother trying to reason with a caveman?" I ask no one in particular.

Wolfgang cheerfully grinds his incisors.

Meine Liebe, I prefer standing on your shoulders when they are not covered by clothes. It makes my paws feel like I'm standing in warm mozzarella.

Turning away from Michael, I hurry down the corridor, and he lets me lead until we get to the exit doors, which is when he goes ahead and roars at the media crowd—or at least that's what it sounds like.

Usually a brave lot, the journalists make a path that is wide enough for a marching band to parade through.

Grunting something unintelligible, Michael takes my elbow and leads me through, while I do my best not to swoon from his touch in front of all these cameras.

Or maybe I should swoon? We are, after all, supposed to make the world think—

"That's yours, right?" Wrinkling his nose, he gestures at my Beetle.

I glare at him. "Now you don't like my car?"

"It doesn't look very safe," he says. "Also, I'm pretty sure it was modeled after one of Hitler's ideas."

What? I got it secondhand from my cousin who is a clown—literally, that is—and I've always associated this type of car with clowns. And sure, they sometimes seem a little evil, but not Hitler-level evil.

"What car do *you* drive?" I ask challengingly.

He points at a sleek muscle car nearby. "A Ford Mustang Shelby GT500."

Damn it. That is the coolest car I've ever seen, and I can't think of anything negative to say about it. Then again... "Looks like the type of ride men get to compensate for something." I make the pinky on my right hand go limp.

"Oh, I have nothing to compensate for." He smiles dangerously. "Would you like confirmation?"

Was that a proposition? My gaze darts at the bulge in his pants, and I swallow thickly. "This conversation is over."

He cocks his head. "Shouldn't we do something for the cameras?"

I swallow again. "Like what?"

He closes the distance between us. "Like this." He takes my face into his hands and kisses me, ruthlessly, like I belong to him.

My panties go the way of the Wicked Witch of the West when doused with a bucket of water—they full-on melt, and so do I.

In the distance, I hear cameras click, and the sounds remind me that this is just for show.

Fuming, I push him away.

"See you tomorrow," he says.

"Go suck a dick."

He actually smiles at that, and his smile is as panty-melting as his kiss. "The Russian expression is go '*to*' the dick. Not 'suck' a dick."

"And the difference is?"

"'Go to the dick' almost literally translates to 'go to hell.'"

I arch an eyebrow. "So you're saying your dick is hell?"

"No, *ptichka*," he murmurs. "For you, my dick will be heaven."

CHAPTER 10
CALLIOPE

When I get home in my Hitler-inspired car, the first thing I do is reunite Wolfgang with the rest of the rat pack. Then I fix all of us some food.

Once Lenin is done eating a frozen grape, he starts doing zoomies around the whole apartment.

Tovarisch, this is the food of the bourgeoisie, and it is having its corrupting influence on the proletari-rat .

Ignoring his antics, I stare at myself in the mirror long and hard.

"The kiss was just for the pictures," I remind myself.

"But then why did it feel so good?" my mirror self asks very reasonably.

"Because you're a dummy. Because you're not careful with—"

My phone rings, which is just as well because if I talk to myself any longer, my rats will have me committed.

It's a video call from Seraphina.

I accept it with a smile. For a change, she's not hanging from the ceiling.

"Hey, former roomie," I say. "Miss me already?"

"Yeah, right. I just need to get up to speed because all your other siblings are inundating me with questions about you and your hockey player."

"*My* other siblings?" I let the "my hockey player" bit slide. "Don't you mean *our*?"

She flashes the super-healthy teeth that she allegedly inherited from our great-great-grandfather, the one famous for his razor-blade chewing and sword swallowing. "Semantics. Now, spill."

"There's nothing to spill," I state.

"Yeah. Right. You're blushing. Did you boink him already?"

I roll my eyes. "Even *you* are not that slutty."

"Just tell me." She makes puppy eyes. "I can't *bear* the suspense anymore."

Should I tell her about the arrangement we've been forced into? Nobody said we had to keep it a secret from our families. In fact, I don't want my family to think this is for real, and telling Seraphina the truth is the same thing as sending them all an email outlining what's happened.

I take a breath. "Fine. We kissed again, but—"

She squeals so loudly the ears of all my rats perk up. "I knew pestering you for info would *bear* fruit."

"As I was about to say, it was just for the cameras." Marco and Polo scurry over, so I pet them both.

She cocks her head. "Why would you kiss him for the cameras?"

I explain that the viral video is a financial boon for the Florida Bears, and that Michael and I are getting paid to keep the public's interest going. Not sure why, but I also mention the small skates he had handy, clearly for the daintily feminine feet of his many puck bunnies.

"Are you sure it's the Florida Bears that *bear* responsibility for that kiss, and not your bear-like boo?"

Am I sure? "This conversation is over."

"Why?" she asks. "Is it because you can't *bear* my bear puns anymore?"

"No, but they do not help," I grumble.

"Please, *bear* with me," she says. "I'm going to run out of them sooner or later."

"I doubt you will run out."

"You've got a point. I'm just getting my *bear*ings."

"I've got to go." I hover my thumb over the "end call" button.

"Wait," she says urgently. "Use a condom when you do boink him. You're of child-*bear*ing age, after all."

I end the call just as she defines a condom for me as a type of *bear*-ier made of latex.

———

The next day, I start practicing the shtick that I plan to unveil for my first game as the Bears' mascot: the Yetis exhibition game in New York.

Inspired by the hatred I'm starting to develop for the press, my main priority will be photobombing. That means as soon as any camera zooms in on a player, or on a fan, I'll jump into the frame and strike a funny pose, and if all goes well, Wolfgang will strike a similar pose to mine. The problem with photobombing is that it is difficult to practice, so I focus on something easy: Mr. Bloom's new ice dance.

Thus far, the dance—and I use this term very loosely —involves pretending to be a T-Rex, roping people in with an invisible lasso, and acting like an octopus that's about to be killed by a sushi chef. Oh, and on occasion, I throw in the classic clown move of slipping on a banana peel, and toward the end, I shuffle around like a zombie.

When I finish the dance, there's a familiar slow clap behind me that I should have expected but didn't.

Executing an elegant spin on the ice, I take advantage of the fact that he can't see where I'm looking when I have the mask on and let my eyes roam freely over his visage. Damn him. Why is he, of all people, so fucking hot? It's not just the rippling muscles or his piercing eyes.

It's his hair. From the stray chest hair peeking through his shirt to the dark, rumpled locks on his head. Oh, and last but not least—as far as my libido is concerned—is his facial hair. As if to taunt me, he hasn't shaved since I saw him yesterday, and what was a five o'clock shadow has become a starter beard.

Wait. As much as I appreciate the feast for the eyes, why would he grow one? After all, a beard is only one letter 'd' away from 'bear.'

"I was becoming concerned for your sanity," Michael states.

I take off the bear mask just so that I can glare at him properly. "My sanity isn't any of your concern. Nothing about me is."

He blows out a breath. "I was just joking."

"That wasn't a joke. But this is: what color socks am I wearing?"

He darts a glance at my feet. "It's difficult to see."

"Wrong," I say. "I'm not wearing any. I have *bear* feet." Yes, Seraphina has rubbed off on me.

He doesn't so much as chuckle—probably because the forbidden topic of bears has been broached. "I think it's smart that you're preparing. Ted just made shit up as he went along, and it was never as professional-looking as that dance."

"Wait. Was that a compliment?" I glance at Wolfgang. "Is the universe about to implode?"

Wolfgang makes a chattering sound by grinding his incisors.

Meine Liebe, at the moment, galaxies are rushing away from each other, which implies that the universe shouldn't implode for a while, if ever. I theorize that the galaxies are chasing supermassive black holes made of the most delectable cheese.

"Are you ready for me to escort you out?" Michael asks gruffly.

"Fine. Let's go," I say with an eyeroll and swing by my changing room before I stride out, feeling his eyes on my back.

With every step, my heartbeat skyrockets in anticipation of what might happen in the parking lot.

After all, we kissed for the cameras yesterday, so we should do so again today, right?

For consistency's sake, of course. It has nothing to do with that beard.

Once again, the media people are still there when we exit, and they scream questions at us that are cut short by Michael's suggestion that everyone go to the fucking dick.

As soon as the journalists have been scared into giving us a path through, Michael takes my elbow and leads me to the parking lot—which makes me feel like I'm floating.

As we approach my Beetle, he releases my elbow.

"See you tomorrow," he murmurs.

I blink at him. "Aren't you forgetting something?"

He arches one of his sexily thick eyebrows. "What am I forgetting?"

I gesture at the journalists. "A kiss?"

He looks like he's just bypassed all bee defenses and is about to savor some premium honey. "You don't think they took enough kissy pictures yesterday?"

I dampen my dry lips. "It's not about the pictures this time. It's about them seeing us being intimate, or not." Yeah. That's why we should do it. "We don't want someone to write a story about how we've already broken up."

He leans in, his lips tantalizingly close. "Are you sure it's for them? Maybe you *want* me to kiss you."

I all but turn into a growly bear myself. "Not if you were the last man on Earth."

He shrugs. "I guess we can fake a kiss for them." He

turns his back to the journalists and envelops me in a hug, but his lips are a whole inch away from mine—which might as well be a mile. "This way they'll think we're kissing," he whispers. "But we're not."

My heart is pounding way too fast, and I feel oddly shivery despite the Florida heat. "But what if someone has a long-focus lens and is hiding where they have just the right angle?" I whisper, then mentally kick myself.

He's going to tease me again. I just know it.

"If someone takes a picture of this, they'll have a picture of us embracing," he murmurs. "In what world does that lead them to conclude that we've broken up?"

How dare he use common sense and logic? I push him away. "I'm going home."

He blows me a mocking air kiss. "Pleasant dreams, *ptichka*."

———

I wake up in the middle of the night, wet. No, that's an understatement. I need a new, better word for how desperately I need sexual release.

Grr. Bastard. It's like he cursed me when he wished me pleasant dreams—and there I went, dreaming of his naked chest and of running my fingers through the hair there. And that wasn't the worst of it. I felt his beard in that dream, both as we kissed and as he went down under—a glorious experience, if only in my imagination.

———

Mom calls as I drive to work and tells me that journalists are hounding the circus, hoping for a sighting of me.

"It's great for business," she says. "We're all probably going to get raises thanks to you."

"Happy to be of service. I'm just hoping they don't figure out where I currently live and bug me there."

If they do, Michael might want to walk me all the way to my door, and that way lies the possibility that I'll accidentally invite him in, and that his cock will accidentally end up inside me.

"So," Mom says conspiratorially. "Have you taken any cooking lessons yet?"

What? "Why?"

"You've got a new boyfriend," she says. "Everyone knows the way to a man's heart is through his stomach."

That sounds like something a serial killer would say. "Did Seraphina not tell you all?" I ask. "He's not my boyfriend. It's just for show."

"Yeah, right," she says. "I saw the video, and the pictures. If you were that good of an actress, you wouldn't be in the circus. You'd be on Broadway instead."

"I'm *not* in the circus," I remind her. "And I assure you, none of it is real."

"Let's agree to disagree," Mom says.

"This isn't a situation where you can use that phrase."

"Let's agree to disagree twice then."

I nearly run over a goffer tortoise crossing the street.

Fortunately, I brake in time. "I forgot to tell you, I'm driving," I say to Mom as I wait for the tortoise to pass. "It's not safe to multitask like this."

"On that, we're in agreement," she says and hangs up.

On *that* we are? So she still thinks Michael and I are dating? I mean, I know she and Dad want grandchildren, but I didn't realize the desire has gotten so desperate that it's causing her to deny reality.

Whatever.

When I finally get to work, I hold off on changing into my bear suit. I need a few volunteers from the team to help with an idea I have for my shtick, and I'm hoping they'll take me more seriously in street clothing.

So… I make the mistake of watching them practice. Or more specifically, I make the mistake of watching Michael do his drills. His beard is even more noticeable today, and it's all too easy to picture him drilling into me, his cock hard as a hockey stick and his beard pleasantly scratchy on my—

"Hi, Calliope," Coach says, scaring the bearjesus out of me.

"Hello, Coach." I wipe my mouth on the off chance that some of the copious amounts of drool I'm producing has escaped.

"Can I help you with something?" he asks.

"Yeah. Make Michael shave," I blurt.

That way, it will be easier to keep my sanity around him—and reduce bodily fluid production.

Coach grins. "Sorry, but no can do. They never shave before an important game, and I won't get in the way of that. Particularly in Michael's case because when he first joined, he mocked this particular superstition on the grounds of 'too many people are doing it, so how can it give you an edge?' The fact that he's since joined in with them tells me he *really* wants to win the upcoming game."

Did he just say "they?" I look at the rest of the players. Yep. All are indeed unshaven. It's just that Michael is able to grow his beard faster and bushier.

Speaking of Michael, I catch him glaring at me, for no reason at all, so I flip him the bird and turn back to Coach. "I was joking anyway. But I could use some help."

"What can I do?" Coach asks.

"Not sure if I want to do this to you," I say. "Better I get a few volunteers from the team."

"Sure. Go for it." He uses his whistle, and everyone looks our way.

Coach gestures for me to speak.

"I need a few volunteers," I announce.

The bearded faces look at me like I might bite.

"It's for my shtick," I explain. "I'd like to do a bit where I stretch an imaginary rope across the ice, and then some of you will trip over it, as if it were real."

A lot of the dudes nod approvingly—until they hear a low growl, that is.

"I volunteer," Michael states. "And no one else."

I stare at him in disbelief. "Do you not get how volunteering works?"

He skates over. "Do you want me to withdraw my candidacy?"

"No. I'll meet you back here." With an eyeroll, I turn around and head to my dressing room to gear up.

Once the costume is on, I place Wolfgang on my shoulder and examine myself in the mirror to get into character.

"Bearman horny like deer. Roar. Bearman want to come on big boobs of his Pookie-poo for the cameras."

Wolfgang washes his face with his paws.

Meine Liebe, this Bearman person sounds like he just needs regular rations of cheese.

Feeling ready for anything, I return to the rink, where Michael is waiting for me along with Coach.

As I explain what I want to do, Coach grins, but Michael's face is completely impassive, like I'm talking about my income taxes and not a fun prank.

Then, after I make a big deal about setting up the invisible rope across the ice, Michael skates through and very deliberately falls.

"That was terrible," I say. "It needs to look natural. That was just you falling on purpose."

His nostrils flare. "How the fuck do I fall naturally?"

"Like it's an accident." I look at Coach for help.

"Hey, Michael," Coach says, his eyes crinkling. "If this is too childish for you, I'm sure Dante would be happy to help Calliope."

"Over his dead body," Michael growls and turns to me. "Just show me how you want me to fall, and I'll do it that way."

Huh. "Like this." I skate toward the invisible rope, then act as if it were a laser that has chopped off the bottom of my feet. I wail in pain, wave my arms around like I've been attacked by a swarm of bees, then clutch my chest and fall on the ice, twitching as I pretend to expire.

"That was natural?" Michael looks from me to Coach.

"It was inspired," Coach says. "Kids will love it."

"And since when is hockey a sport for kids?" Michael grumbles.

"Didn't you start at four?" Coach counters.

Michael's face turns exceptionally gloomy, even for him. "Let me try the fucking fall." Gritting his teeth in determination, he skates over to the "rope" and then repeats the ridiculous challenge I've set out for him— except he manages to do it with a predatory grace more typical of a feline.

"How?" I ask no one in particular.

"His kinesthetic intelligence is off the charts," Coach says.

I exchange a confused glance with Wolfgang. "Does that mean Michael can read minds?"

Meine Liebe, my mind is easily read. 'Cheese.'

"No." Coach chuckles. "It means he can use his body with great precision."

Was it Coach's intention to give me an onslaught of dirty images, ones where Michael uses his body on me... with great precision? Wait. That makes it sound like my holes are difficult to hit or something, which they—

"How was that?" Michael growls.

"Very... precise," I say. "But not at all funny."

"But the potential is there," Coach says quickly.

"Can you do it again but pretend that you're very drunk?"

Muttering something about everyone going to dicks, Michael tries again, and this time, his fall is hilarity itself.

"There you go," Coach says. "I knew you could do it."

"And you're a good coach, Coach," I add.

Michael stretches his arms—which are probably sore from all that flailing. "Who knew looking like a fucking idiot would be such a challenge."

"But you do it so naturally," I say, flapping my eyelashes at him all innocent-like.

"I walked right into that one, didn't I?" he growls.

"On the bright side," Coach says, "I've been telling you that you need to do more assists, and that was an excellent one."

A female clears her throat behind us. It turns out to be Linda from HR. "I hope I'm not interrupting."

"How much of that did you see?" I ask.

She shudders. "Are you asking if I saw our most expensive player nearly break his neck?"

Most expensive? Do hockey players get paid proportionally to their grouchiness?

"What do you want?" Michael demands.

She shuffles from foot to foot. "I wanted to run something by you both. An idea from PR." She winces. "It has to do with your accommodations in New York."

"What about them?" I ask.

Linda wipes a bead of sweat from her forehead.

"They—we—wanted to know if you two would be okay sharing a hotel room."

I feel like my brain has just tripped over the invisible rope and is flailing its hippocampus and hypothalamus as it lands on its amygdala. "Me and him?" I point at Michael. "Or him and Coach?"

Coach raises his hands like I've got a gun pointed at his chest. "I'm staying with my wife. Sorry."

"Why the fuck?" Michael demands.

"To further fuel the rumors," Linda says. "Otherwise, the press may start to question whether you're really together. The two of you haven't been seen together much, so…"

I glare at her. "I'm not doing it."

"Me neither," Michael says, his black eyes glinting with wrath.

"It will be a room with two beds," Linda squeals. "With a partition between them as well."

"Aren't those partitions made from paper and wood?" I slant a glance at Michael's crotch for no reason at all. "I'm not exactly reassured."

Michael doesn't reply, but his expression makes Linda take a step back.

"Mr. Ironside—the team owner—is willing to give both of you a bonus for the inconvenience," she says in a loud whisper. "Twenty percent of your annual salaries." She faces Michael. "He also said he would donate a hundred times that to your—"

"Deal," Michael growls and turns to me. "I will, of course, be a perfect gentleman."

"Fine," I say, probably because my brain is still on

the fritz. "I'll do it." That money will go a long way toward my rat show dream.

As Linda runs away, I narrow my eyes at Michael. "What's he donating money toward?"

"I have to change," he says, ignoring my question. "Where do you want to meet so we can exit together?"

"By the front doors?"

With a nod, he strides away.

I turn to Coach. "Do you know what the money is for?"

"I do," Coach says. "But it's Michael's secret project, so you'll have to get him to tell you. Sorry."

Secret project? "Does he run a bear preservation society?" That's something a rich guy might want to donate money to.

Coach shakes his head. "Please don't put me in this position."

"Fine. I guess I'll go change."

Coach looks relieved, which is why I don't offer him my second guess: a high-tech facility where toys, porn, and zebras are cleverly utilized to encourage giant pandas to mate.

CHAPTER 11
MICHAEL

"You okay?" Dante asks me when I storm into the locker room.

I slam my locker door, hard. "Those fucking fucks want me and Calliope to stay in the same hotel room in New York."

Dante snorts. "You and the girl you like spending a night together. The horror."

I whirl on him. "Don't fucking test me. On top of that, fucking Linda almost told Calliope about my secret project."

He shrugs. "Would it be so bad if she knew? She might actually like you more."

"Fuck." I rip off my jersey.

"She may do that too, if she knew about—"

"Shut the fuck up," I hiss at Dante because Jack comes out of the showers—and he's not in on my secret, and never will be.

"She could even help," Dante says vaguely. "If I were you, I'd take her to the fundraiser when—"

"Which part of 'shut the fuck up' did you not get?" I growl.

Then again, his idea is worth considering. Not that she'd agree to accompany me to any events.

Changing quickly, I rush downstairs, where I wait for what seems like hours for Calliope to show up.

"Finally," I can't help but say when she appears.

"I could make my own way to the car," she retorts.

Not dignifying that with a response, I open the door and channel my frustration at the fuckers outside.

Unfortunately for my itching fists, they make way for us, so I take *ptichka* by her elbow and lead her through the parking lot—ready to punch anyone who asks us some stupid question. Here again, I don't get the chance.

Speaking of people I'd punch… "Have you seen any other signs of your stalker?"

She shakes her head. "We don't know that it was a stalker, but no." Yet she looks a little unsure.

"There's something else, isn't there?"

She hesitates. "Now that I think about it, when I got to my place on my first day, something seemed off. There were some smudges on the walls, and a few floorboards looked like they'd been pulled up and then placed back."

"Fucking stalker," I growl.

"Or it was my imagination," she says. "Also, I'm not sure the video was even viral yet at that time."

I clench and unclench my fist. "Do you have a security system?"

"No."

"I'm going to make some calls. One is getting installed tonight."

She rolls her eyes. "That sounds like overkill."

"It's better to have a security system and never need it."

"Whatever." Her classically shaped nose wrinkles. "Now… can you tell me what your secret project is?"

I lean in. "Can you keep a secret?"

She nods eagerly and gets so close I can almost taste her lips.

"So can I," I say and watch as the disappointment spreads over her face.

"Fine," she says. "I'm going." Yet she doesn't move even an inch. A flap of a butterfly's wing is all it would take to have our lips meet.

My heart pounds heavily, and my voice is a touch too husky as I say, "Don't we have some pretending to do?"

Her shoulders dip fetchingly. "Not everyone kisses their girlfriend goodbye every day."

"If you were really mine, I would."

Fuck, what am I saying? Why am I saying it? It's like a demon has taken hold of my tongue. Or my dick.

She moistens her lips. "Seems like we don't have much of a choice."

The demon pushes me from behind, making me dip my head, and my lips clash against hers.

Her breathy gasp of surprise tells me that she didn't expect it—but she doesn't push me away. No, she returns the kiss with a passion that could win her an Oscar.

I pull her closer and she melts into me, her soft parts driving my hard ones insane.

The sound of cameras clicking brings me back to reality, and I pull away from her.

Eyes wild, she touches her lips. "I bet that was pretty convincing."

I nod. "See you tomorrow, *ptichka*."

With that, I drag myself away and drive home in a haze. When I get there, two journalists are waiting for me, and one asks about Calliope.

I destroy his camera first, then do the same to the other asshole. Then I promise to break body parts if I see them again and head into my house.

Finally. I'm still painfully hard after that kiss, so I fist my dick to release the tension. Afterward, I eat dinner and get on my computer to work on my secret project.

By the time my eyes grow tired from staring at the monitor, I have a new sponsor secured and have managed to score an invitation to a fundraiser where I can meet more while I'm in New York. It's a black-tie event, so I go over to the suitcase I've already prepared and pack my tux into it.

The problem is, just dressing the part isn't going to help me score more sponsors. I'll need to shmooze and be fucking polite, which isn't my forte.

Maybe I should ask Calliope to join me. Despite being a contrarian who would no doubt have a rat on her shoulder even at a black-tie event, she'd do a much better job than I ever could when it comes to charming people. Something about her just draws you in. Some sort of a sparkle, for lack of a better term, and I don't just mean the color of her nails.

But no. I can't. It sounds too much like an actual date. And it would feel like one too, which is the last thing we need.

Closing my computer, I walk over to my telescope and unwind by watching the hawk family.

———

The next day, by the end of the practice, I realize I've almost lost my voice from yelling at my sorry excuses for teammates.

Sweating bullets, I approach Coach while he is speaking with Calliope, and catch her asking, "Maybe you should enroll him in anger management classes?"

"Fuck that," I growl. "But you *could* enroll these lazy fuckers in some 'intro to hockey' classes."

Coach turns my way. "I know you want to win, but maybe you're pushing yourself and the others a little too hard?"

I narrow my eyes at him. "Shouldn't you want us to win more than I do, Coach?"

"It's an exhibition game," he reminds me. "A glorified practice. There's no prize money. No impact on rankings. It doesn't count toward anything."

I shake my head vehemently. "After we beat them, my prize will be the expressions on their faces." Especially one specific face.

"*If* we beat them," Coach says. "Our chances aren't that good. They're a much stronger team and—"

"Which is why they're going to be overconfident," I say. "And not try their hardest—for all the reasons you've mentioned."

"So why do *you* want to beat them so much?" Calliope asks just as Dante skates over and takes off his mask, nearly blinding us all with his paleness.

"Because they fired him," Dante says without missing a beat. "And it's not just all of them that he wants to defeat, but Mason Tugev especially. The one responsible for said firing."

I restrain all of my violent urges. Dante is a friend. Plus he's an outstanding goalie, and we need him for the game in question. "Tugev actually claimed it was their coach who fired me," I grit out. "The real reason I want to beat him is because he thinks he's the best in the league."

"He and the rest of the world," Dante says. "Present company excluded, of course."

"Mason Tugev," Calliope repeats with a frown. "Isn't that guy a billionaire?"

"Exactly," I say grimly. "And all that money has made him soft, I'm sure."

"He's the team owner now," Coach adds. "So he's probably thinking about retirement rather than winning."

"There you go," I say. "This might be my last chance to best him."

"Don't you mean for *your* team to best *his* team?" Coach asks with a smirk.

"I'm sure he meant exactly what he said," Calliope

says with an eyeroll. "The man's ego is the size of Mount Everest."

Dante gives her a high five, and I almost break his arm for daring to touch her—friend/goalie or not. What stops me is Coach's hand on my shoulder.

The man understands me much better than anyone else.

"So, Calliope," Coach says. "Any new shenanigans you need help with?" The bastard looks pointedly at me.

"Actually, yes," she says. "But I'm not sure if I should clear them with everyone, or just run with them."

"Clear it with *him*," Dante and Coach say in unison, looking at me.

"Especially if you're planning them for the Yetis game," Coach adds.

She sighs. "Okay. I was planning on attacking you with a giant foam finger after you score."

"You have furry paws," Dante says. "How are you going to hold onto a giant foam finger?"

"That's my burden to *bear*," she says.

I grit my teeth. "Fine. You can use the finger." But only because the plan takes it for granted that I *will* score.

She chuckles. "I'll call this bit 'Michael gets fingered.'"

Coach and Dante laugh uproariously, and my only non-violent option becomes to turn on my heel and leave.

When I walk out of the locker room, Calliope is waiting for me, and she looks extra delectable now that the bulky mascot suit isn't hiding her curves.

"Hey," she says. "Are you mad?"

"Mad as in insane?"

I did, after all, agree to pretend to date this woman.

"Mad as in angry," she says with a slight eyeroll. "You were being unnaturally agreeable when you said yes to—let's call it Project Foam Finger—and I made a joke at your expense instead of saying thanks."

"Unnaturally agreeable?" I arch an eyebrow. "You might just be worse at apologies than I am."

"Sorry. Now, can we go?"

"Sure." As if possessed, I take her elbow right then —without any journalists in sight. If she minds, she doesn't show it, so we walk like that all the way to her car.

"So…" She nods at the idiots with cameras and bites her lower lip. "Shall we?"

Oh, yes. I kiss her once more, the taste of cotton candy as intoxicating as it is arousing. The world around us seems to fade away, at least until she gently steps back from me—at which point I hear the clicks of cameras over the hammering of my heartbeat.

"See you tomorrow," she says shyly.

The best I can do as far as replies go is a grunt. But hey, it could have been worse.

I could have growled.

———

The next few days blur together. I practice like my life depends on winning, and then I kiss Calliope for the cameras with a similar fervor and without a care for how blue my balls get. After that, I jerk off, work on fundraising, look at the hawks, and sleep, then rinse and repeat.

"So…" Calliope says after we grudgingly disconnect from the kiss on the day of our flight. "I'll see you on the plane, right?"

"Correct." I doubt it was necessary, but I've already warned my teammates that I'm sitting next to her, and that they'd better stay away on the pain of… a lot of pain. "Why do you ask? Did you want to watch a movie together?"

Her eyes light up. "Could we?"

"Sure. What kind of movies do you like?"

She darts a glance at Wolfgang. "*Ratatouille* is my favorite, but I also like *Encanto*—because of Bruno's friends."

Thanks to my secret project, I'm actually familiar with the movies in question, so I ask, "Are we allowed to talk about Bruno?"

Her eyes widen. "You're right. We don't talk about Bruno. No. No. No."

I resist the urge to kiss her again. "So… do the movies you like always have rats?"

She shakes her head. "I like *Stuart Little*, and he's a mouse."

"Ah. You like rodents then."

She shakes her head again. "I like Pikachu, and he's a Pokémon—a fictional creature with superpowers."

"Yeah, but he still looks rodent-like."

She narrows her eyes. "How are you so up to speed on things that kids like? Do you have any of your own?"

"Nope."

"Nieces or nephews?"

"No." The word comes out more growly than I intend. "I don't have *any* family." Fucking fuck. How did we get on to this subject?

She gapes at me. "Any?"

"No. I grew up in a Russian orphanage—and the less said about that, the better." Else I might just go berserker on the nearby media fucks, and that wouldn't be good for the team's PR.

"I'm sorry," she whispers, staring up at me. "I didn't know."

I feel a muscle pulse in my jaw. "Can we change the subject?"

"Yeah. Sure. Let's just finish talking about movies. What kinds do you like? Maybe we can find one that we'd both enjoy?"

"I like movies with spies and superheroes," I say. "My favorite character is Black Widow."

She rolls her eyes. "Is it because you think Scarlett Johansson is hot?"

"No. I relate to her character's backstory."

Shit. Why did I just say that?

When Calliope stares at me like I've grown a second head, I'm forced to explain. "Born in Russia, recruited into a grueling training program. The only difference is the curriculum: spying versus hockey."

She just continues staring at me, her face a kaleido-scope of emotions. "So, when Coach said you started hockey at four, it wasn't voluntary?"

"It wasn't, but I grew to like hockey pretty soon after that, and I understood that my life would be much worse without it. Still, being trained using Soviet-era methods is not something I'd recommend, even to my enemies."

She takes my hand into hers, her small palm soft and warm around my fingers. "I'm sorry... again."

"It's fine." I nod toward the journalists. "They're probably getting some great pictures of us having a heart to heart, so there's that."

"Yeah," she says and releases my hand.

I mourn the loss of her touch, but I can't tell her that. "Have any movie suggestions?" I ask instead.

She nods. "How about *The Suicide Squad*?"

I cock my head. "The old or the new one?"

I heard the older version sucks.

"Only the newer one has the 'the' in the title," she says. "And it's the only one that has Ratcatcher 2, a character who likes rats as much as I do."

"No spoilers," I say gruffly. "I haven't seen it."

"Oh." She smiles. "You're in for a treat."

Fuck. Why does it all of a sudden feel like we're going on a movie date? What's worse, we can't even tell ourselves this is part of the usual ruse since we'll be in the air, so no one except my team will see this, and they already believe we're a couple.

"Would it be a good idea to kiss again?" Calliope

asks shyly. "I figure that's what a real couple would do after a heart to heart."

Good idea? Hell, no. But I draw her to me anyway and kiss her with everything I've got.

CHAPTER 12
CALLIOPE

On the commute home and during the ride to the airport, I reflect on what I've learned about Michael today—and enrich this information with whatever tidbits I can locate online. Apparently, as a newborn, he was left on the doorstep of an orphanage in Novosibirsk, which is a town in Siberia, a part of Russia that's famous for being so cold and dark that you could punish people by sending them into exile there. At four years of age, Michael was discovered by a hockey coach due to his aptitude for the sport. He had an entire hockey career as a teen back in Russia, and when he became an adult, he moved to the United States.

Being part of an extremely large and boisterous family, I can't imagine growing up without them. Nor can I imagine living in a place as cold as Novosibirsk. Their warmest day happens to be just below the temperature we'd get on the coldest day here in Florida, so I shudder to think what their winter is like.

One thing Michael and I do share is the fact that someone trained us early in life, but in my case, it was a pretty gentle training, all things considered.

So yeah, Michael clearly had a difficult early life, which may explain some of his grouchiness.

My heart aches as I picture him as a little boy, with black soulful eyes and the earliest mustache in history. If I had a time machine, I'd—

The car stops, interrupting my thoughts. The door opens to reveal Michael in all his glory.

My already overworked heart does a backflip. The man is wearing a muscle shirt, as well as shorts that expose his powerful and scrumptiously hairy legs. Oh, and he's even neatened his beard.

"No," he says sternly to the driver, who has just opened the trunk. "I'm getting her bags."

While he brings over my suitcase, I grab my rat carrier from the seat next to me and get out.

"How many rats do you have in there?" Michael asks, staring at my carrier.

"Six," I reply. "The ones you haven't met are Lenin, Marco, Polo, Damon, and Catnip."

"Lenin?" Michael arches an eyebrow. "Is that after—"

"A comrade from your motherland." I point at Lenin, so he notices the uncanny resemblance.

"Why?" Michael asks.

Huh. I guess he can't see it. "He grew up to resemble his namesake, but even as a pup, he seemed like a commie—always unhappy with how many treats I'd give him, and treat distribution in general. I thought about naming him Karl, after Marx, but then I would've had two rats with German names."

"You have Marco and Polo. Aren't those two Italian names?"

I sigh. "Marco and Polo are identical twins, so… I think that allows for an exception." I mean, I assume they're identical twins. They came from the same litter and look and act exactly alike.

He studies the rats in the carrier with fascination. "All six of them look identical to me."

"Wow. That's a pretty ratist thing to say."

He rolls his eyes. "Ready to board?"

I nod and we get onto the private jet, which is to commercial planes what first class is to coach. The seats are bigger than my lounge chair at home, and there's enough space around each of them for a man of Michael's size to spread out comfortably.

"Here." Michael gestures at an adjacent pair of seats near Coach and Dante. "Sit there."

I do, and before I can comment on how comfy the cushion is, he descends into his seat and presses some button that makes our seats join together, turning them into a makeshift loveseat.

Are his teammates giggling?

Michael slants them a glare, and they all go quiet.

"We're watching *The Suicide Squad*," Michael announces. "Anyone have a problem with that?"

No one admits to having a problem with it, though Dante does mutter something about it not being the most romantic movie.

"Can I get you something to drink?" asks a flight

attendant who clearly works nights as a ninja and weekends as a super model.

"Tomato juice," Michael replies.

"Non-alcoholic," she says approvingly, then bats her ridiculously long lashes at him. "You've got that important game tomorrow."

Seriously? "I will have a Bloody Mary," I say very pointedly.

Given the expression on the woman's perfect face, you'd think she really hadn't noticed me until that second. "Sure," she says offhandedly. Turning back to Michael, she croons, "Would you like salt in your juice?"

Oh, come on. What about asking me how much vodka I want in my drink, or how much hot sauce and so on? Also, I have a funny feeling she plans to include spit in it, or even a splash of cyanide.

To his credit, Michael just grunts in the negative without so much as gracing her with a glance.

"Would you like anything else?" she asks in a tone that implies her pussy is on the list of offerings.

Michael looks at me, and it has to be my overactive imagination, but the corners of his lips seem to lift, as though in a hint of a smile. "Do your rats need a drink?"

"Rats?" The flight attendant's eyes grow so big she wouldn't look out of place in an anime.

I present the carrier to her the way Rafiki did with Simba.

What happens to the flight attendant is best described by the expression "a fit of the vapors." She screams like a horny banshee, goes paler than Dante, and then climbs Coach like a tree.

"My rats are harmless," I say after the shrieking subsides. "And they're inside the carrier."

For now, at least. I'm considering letting them out to stretch their legs, but between possible turbulence and so many giant hockey players around, I'm not sure I'll risk it.

One of the pilots comes out, along with another flight attendant—a woman who is even more attractive than the hysterical one.

"What seems to be the problem?" the pilot demands.

I show them both my carrier. "I think she's afraid of my emotional support animals."

Both the pilot and the other flight attendant react so calmly to the sight of my rats you'd think they meet passengers like me every day.

"Hey, Precious," the pilot says, looking at the flight attendant on top of Coach. "Are you going to be able to get yourself together?"

Precious? Was she named by Gollum?

With a visible effort, Precious climbs off of Coach and shakes her head.

A kerfuffle ensues during which Precious is swapped for someone who is a lot less ratphobic. Meanwhile, the hockey players tease Coach for being flustered after being assaulted by a woman who isn't his wife.

"Sorry, everyone," I say when the jokes at Coach's expense subside. "I didn't mean to delay us."

"Don't worry about it," Dante says. "She tried to

flirt with your man, so you had to unleash a plague of rats on her. It's only logical."

I frown. "The collective noun for rats is a pack."

"Isn't it a swarm?" Kangaroo Jack chimes in.

"Pack," I say firmly.

"A plague is a group of locusts," Coach says, clearly pleased with the change of topic.

"Precious is lucky she left before the movie started," I say. "There's—"

"No spoilers," Michael growls. "In fact, why don't we start the fucking movie before someone ruins it."

In reply, a big screen scrolls down in front of us, and the film studio logo appears.

Midway through the first scene, we are ordered to buckle up for departure. As soon as we are allowed to unbuckle, Michael scoots over and envelops me in his big arm, short-circuiting my brain.

I refuse all drinks and food offered to me and don't remind anyone about the Bloody Mary because I can't be sure it will not contain Precious's spit—or worse. I feel grateful I've seen this movie before because I doubt that I would remember anything about it other than the warmth of Michael's arm. Not warmth, heat. Said arm remains slung over my shoulder all the way until the credits roll, by which point my ovaries have released a dozen eggs that are now all sunny side up in my uterus.

"Isn't it suspicious that we're landing just as the movie ends?" Dante asks.

"Coincidence," Coach says. "This movie is two hours and some change, and so is the flight from Florida to New York."

Everyone discusses this while Michael and I sneak out and jump into one of the waiting limos.

Once inside the vehicle, despite the obscene amount of room, we sit next to each other, so close, in fact, that I feel tingly again.

"I really enjoyed that movie," he says as we get going. "Thank you."

Movie? What movie? All I remember is his arm around my body, and waves upon waves of happy hormones.

I clear my inexplicably dry throat. "Are you feeling ready for the game tomorrow?"

He nods. "I'm going to crush Tugev."

I chuckle. "Great. That totally doesn't sound like something an evil villain would say. Not at all."

He shrugs. "As you just saw in that movie, the line between villain and hero can be thin."

Before I can reply, Wolfgang produces a short squeak from the rat carrier.

"Ah, right." I take him out and allow him to perch on my shoulder. "Good job being patient until now."

Wolfgang blinks at me.

Meine Liebe, the proper way to show your appreciation is with a generous serving of cheese.

"Fine," I tell him. "I'll order a cheese plate when we get to the hotel."

The pack chirps excitedly. They seem to have learned the "c" word.

"You speak to them?" Michael asks. He doesn't sound disapproving, like my ex was, merely curious.

I smile sheepishly. "They're my friends."

"I think I get it," he says.

I examine him skeptically. "You do?"

"Why not?" he demands. "You still think I'm some sort of monster?"

Wolfgang's ears perk up. He must've heard "Munster."

"It's just that you've never mentioned any pets," I say.

"When was I supposed to mention it?" he demands. "After you slammed a pie in my face? Or after you made me play dead—like a fucking dog?"

I roll my eyes. "You forgot 'after being molested with a giant foam finger.'"

"I didn't forget," he growls. "The foam finger is something that's in my bright future—but I'm sure you'll ask me all sorts of personal questions afterward."

"Hey, you started it," is the most mature retort that I can come up with. "Plus, you don't let me prank anyone else but you."

"Whatever," he says gruffly. He waits a beat, then admits, "I don't have any pets."

I squint. "But there's something. I can tell."

"No pets," he says again, but he sounds strangely hesitant.

"What about an aquarium?" I demand. "One with a spiny lumpsucker inside?" It's a fish one of my cousins owns, and I've never seen a creature that looks so much like its name, and its owner.

"I don't have any fucking pets," he grits out. "I just watch birds."

He's a bird watcher? I never would have guessed that in a million years. "What kinds of birds?"

"All kinds."

I smile. "So… penguins? Ostriches?"

His jaw ticks. "I watch them in the wild, not in some fucking zoo."

"Ah, so Florida birds?"

He nods. "White ibises, scrub-jays, wood storks, painted buntings, snail k—"

I chuckle. "Do you specialize in birds with funny names?"

"No. I was giving them to you in order of how common they are."

Wow. He's *really* into this. "Why don't you get a bird as a pet?"

"Because birds are meant to fly. How is that supposed to work indoors?"

I shrug. "Maybe rescue a bird that lost a wing or something?"

He looks thoughtful, then shakes his head. "I prefer watching them in their natural habitat." He hesitates, then adds, "There's actually a hawk family I've been watching recently."

I arch an eyebrow. "How do you know that they're a family?"

"I saw them build a nest, and then she laid just the one egg," he says, his expression darkening. "It should have been somewhere between three and six."

"Wow," I say. "It sounds like you've gotten attached."

"No," is his growled—and unconvincing—reply.

"Did you name them?"

His jaw twitches. "What the fuck does that prove?"

"So that's a yes," I say triumphantly. "What *are* their names?"

He frowns. "Ethan and Mo are the parents, and Eye is the chick."

They are totally his pet hawks. They just live outdoors. Then I fully register the names and grin like a loon. "A hawk named Eye? Is that after Hawkeye, Black Widow's best friend?"

The frown is replaced with a hint of a smile that touches his eyes, which is all the confirmation I need.

"And the parents are Mo Hawk and Ethan Hawk?"

Now the smile touches his yummy lips—which you can barely see under the beard. "Let's hope the hawks never meet your best friends because they'd eat them."

I wave that away. "My rats live indoors." And that isn't such an unnatural habitat for them.

"You sure?" He gestures at Wolfgang.

I scowl. "If some stupid bird tried to go after him, I'd break its stupid beak."

Michael's stomach rumbles, loudly. "I should've had some food on the plane."

"Actually, I'm hungry too." For those hidden lips… but food would be helpful as well.

He knocks on the partition that separates us from the driver. When the partition descends, he asks the driver what there is to snack on in this car, and the menu turns out to be that of a fancy restaurant—and includes a cheese plate.

Closing the partition, I let the rats out so they can feast alongside us.

Michael doesn't seem to mind at all.

"You know," he says as he raises a cracker with caviar to his mouth. "I told you about my family situation—or lack thereof—but you never told me about yours."

Ah. That. I'm worried that if he learns about my family, he will not want to even pretend to date me anymore. Then again, if he's like that, fuck him. I don't want to date him either. Fake date, I mean.

So, as I devour the fancy appetizers, I tell him about growing up in the circus and list some of the more outrageous "jobs" of my family members.

"Wait," he says after I mention my grandparents. "Were you joking, or was your Pop-Pop really a human cannonball?"

That's where he thought I was joking? Not when I mentioned a cousin who has a regurgitation act?

"No, I'm serious. Pop-Pop got shot out of a cannon until he retired. Oh, and his act has been retired too." I grin. "They couldn't find another man of his caliber." In case it wasn't clear, I add, "That part was a joke."

Michael groans. "All the best comedians tell people that they've just made a joke."

"There are more jokes where that one came from," I tell him.

He arches a sexy, bushy eyebrow.

"Do you know what you call the act of eating a member of my family?"

He shakes his head.

"I'll give you a clue. Why wouldn't you want to eat a member of my family?"

He looks at me like I might require psychiatric help. "Because… cannibalism?"

"Wrong. The respective answers are: 'tossing the salad' and 'because we taste funny.'"

"I don't get it," he says. "Or is that on purpose?"

"Come on. Our last name is Klaunbut," I say, this time pronouncing it as everyone else does.

"Clown butt?" He cocks his head. "Didn't you say it was 'claw-un-boot?'"

I sigh. "It's clown butt. I just didn't want to give you any more ammunition."

He groans again. "I get it now, though I wish I didn't. Tossing someone's salad is slang for eating butt, and you wouldn't want to eat a clown because they taste funny."

I slow clap and roll my eyes. "Do you think you're better at jokes than I am?"

His eyes go slitty. "A guy gets lost in the woods and starts shouting. A bear walks up to him and asks why he's making all the noise. 'I'm lost,' the guy explains. 'So I was hoping someone would hear me.' The bear bares his teeth. 'I heard you. Feel better now?'"

I suppress a chuckle. "Is this a test?"

He pauses mid-bite of his cracker. "What?"

"You tell a joke that features a bear, I laugh, and then you get pissed off."

He blows out a breath. "You can laugh when I tell a bear joke. Just don't call me a bear."

"Deal," I say, but then I can't help but ask why he's so touchy about it.

So he tells me, and in a weird way, it makes sense. Being a Klaunbut, I can even relate.

"Is that why you hate the mascot?" I tap my suitcase, where Mr. Bloom is vacuum-sealed in a specialized bag.

"I hate the fact that some people call *me* the mascot behind my back."

Oh. "Who?" And are they suicidal?

He clenches and unclenches his fist. "Russian-speaking players from other teams."

"That can't be many people." Yet it explains why he's broken so many noses on the ice.

"Ten percent of the league are Russian," he counters. "Plus, there are plenty like Tugev who aren't Russian but speak the language enough to mock me."

Wow. "That's more than I would expect."

"Oh, it's nothing. There are four times as many Canadians." He wipes his hands on his napkin.

I wipe mine too. "That makes more sense."

"Yeah," he says. "Dante is Canadian."

"He is? I would have guessed Transylvanian."

This time, Michael smiles full-on, with teeth showing and everything, and it's a glorious event, like a sunrise over a stormy ocean.

As if it's developed a mind of its own, my hand lands on his thigh. "I will not make any bear jokes ever again."

His eyes grow heated. "And I will never start making clown butt ones."

I scoot closer to him. "It's a deal."

He leans toward me. "A deal has to be properly sealed."

It's unclear who moves first, but our lips meet.

The world starts to fade way... and then our stupid limo stops.

CHAPTER 13
MICHAEL

Fucking fuck. I'm not sure who I'm angrier at: the two of us for deciding to kiss without cameras, or the driver for interrupting it.

"We're here." Calliope touches her luscious lips and clears her throat. "Which is probably for the best."

"Yeah. We shouldn't have done that." It's like eating chocolate-covered bacon—tastes good in the moment but has detrimental effects on your heart.

Calliope's nostrils flare. "We definitely shouldn't have. What were we thinking?"

I blow out a breath. "You just said maybe it's for the best that—"

"And it is. We should only do things like that when someone is watching. Otherwise, what's the point?"

"I fucking concur." Nearly breaking the limo door, I get out and then let my frustration out by snapping at the limo driver and the porter who try to help with Calliope's suitcase.

The fucking media people are here, taking pictures as I carry said suitcase inside.

"Is this why you insist on carrying my stuff?" she asks as we step into the hotel. "For the pictures?"

"Yeah," I grit out. "I can only do something nice in a cold-hearted, calculated manner."

"Please. You're not doing it as a nice gesture. It's just macho posturing."

I decide to be the adult and not reply, which may be the hardest thing I've ever done. Instead, I stride over to the nearest concierge, make sure the rat carrier is not in her sight, and give her our names.

"Ah, right." She grins conspiratorially. "We know who the two of you are, so we upgraded your room." She hands me and Calliope two passkeys and explains how to get to the room in question. "I'm sure you'll enjoy it." She accompanies the last two words with a slight waggle of her drawn-on-with-pencil eyebrows.

Fuck. Until now, I've tried to put the fact that we're sharing a room out of my mind, but the concierge's insinuation—or whatever that was—brings me back to the reality of this situation.

We're going to be breathing the same air. Calliope is going to be in the same shower as—

"Excuse me?" Calliope snaps. "Why did you say 'enjoy it' like that?"

The concierge turns beet red. "Because you're going to have an amazing view? And the—"

"Don't bother." Calliope heads for the elevator without waiting to see if I will follow, and I have to sprint to make it before the doors close.

"Stupid 'close door' button doesn't work," Calliope mutters, seemingly to Wolfgang.

"Very mature," I reply.

Calliope huffs, and we ride to the top floor in silence. A silence that's maintained all the way to the ornate door of our room.

It's not until we step inside that we resume talking —assuming a stream of curses qualifies as such.

"They gave us a honeymoon suite," Calliope says after she runs out of cuss words. Since she speaks only one language, her vocabulary is much more limited in this regard than mine.

I glare at the giant four-poster bed covered in rose petals. "There had better be another place for one of us to sleep."

Her eyes widen, and she runs toward a nearby door.

"That's a bathroom," she says and checks the other door. "And that's a closet."

"So... just one fucking bed?" Given the size of the suite, there could have been another bed in here, but someone put in a useless open dining area instead. There's also a jacuzzi, but sleeping in one is a drowning risk.

"Screw that." She rushes out of the room and back into the elevator, again so fast it's an effort to keep up.

Marching over to the same concierge, she demands we get the original room that was booked for us.

"But why?" The concierge stares at us in confusion. "Your new room is the best one we've got."

"Because she said so," I growl.

The concierge blanches. "I'm sorry. Your original room is no longer available."

"Fine. Give us another room—with two separate beds," Calliope demands. "Or two rooms."

The concierge takes a step back. "I'm sorry. We're the closest hotel to the stadium, and with the game coming up, there are no rooms available."

"Then we'll go to another hotel," Calliope threatens.

"It's nine p.m.," the concierge says. "And the game is tomorrow. Your chances of finding a room are slim to none."

"Also, there's no *we*," I say bluntly. "I'm not going to another hotel."

Calliope whips around to face me. "You're not?"

"I have to go to sleep early the night before a game."

In fact, I plan to call it a night in about an hour.

"Fine," Calliope grits out and rushes back to the fucking suite.

I follow her there.

She stalks from wall to wall, examining our accommodations like another bed might be hiding in plain sight.

"You realize the concierge could tell some journalist about that incident," I tell her. "And that it could start a rumor that we've broken up?"

She narrows her eyes. "Are you saying you *want* to sleep in the same bed?"

"No," I growl. "But who said we have to? I'm fine sleeping on the floor."

She looks down like she's never seen floors before,

then shakes her head. "You're not going to get any sleep that way."

"It's fine. I've slept in much worse conditions." Hell, there's a rug here, something that would have seemed like a luxury back in—

"You've got a game tomorrow," she reminds me.

Fuck.

I cross my arms over my chest. "There's no way you're sleeping on the floor while I'm on the bed."

"We can share it then," she says. "But no funny business."

"Funny business?"

Is she blushing, or are her cheeks red with anger? "No sex," she elaborates. "No touching. No kissing."

I shrug. "You don't have to worry about that. I always stay abstinent the night before a game."

Not to mention, I don't sleep with coworkers, or stubborn women who are as infuriating as—

"How fortuitous." Her words drip with sarcasm. "I take my mascot duties very seriously, so I avoid sex before a game too. I also abstain from speaking with assholes."

With that, she strides toward the bathroom, her hips swaying as if she's trying to get me to notice how amazing her ass is.

And it is fucking amazing. Magnificent, really. I'm not the type to write poetry, but if I were, I'd dedicate a sonnet to this ass.

She locks the door, and I hear the shower come on.

Fuck me. All I can think of is that she's naked in

there, hot water running down her body, that curvy ass sudsy and—

Great. Now I'm painfully hard and can't do anything about it. The pre-game abstinence is about not coming, so jerking off is as much off the table as sex.

After what feels like hours, she comes out of the bathroom, wearing a hotel robe.

"Wolfgang," she says to one of her rats. "Can you tell Michael to not be here as I change into my PJs?"

"Seriously?" I grab a pair of clean boxers, stomp over to the bathroom, and slam the door.

Fucking hell. The place smells like clean feminine flesh, and it makes me even harder—which I didn't think was possible.

I turn the faucet all the way to cold, undress, and step into the shower.

Damn. The last time I was this cold was back in Novosibirsk—and the worst part is that the shower isn't helping on the erection front. Not at all.

Well, I'll just stand here longer.

I wait until I'm shivering, which is when the erection subsides a bit.

Thank fuck.

I get out, brush my teeth, and pull on my boxers.

"Hey, Wolfgang," I shout before opening the door. "Is Calliope decent?"

No reply. Not even a rat squeak.

"I'm coming out."

No one raises any objections.

When I open the door, the suite is dimly lit. The

blinds are closed, blocking all the lights generated by the City That Never Sleeps, but a small lamp in the corner is turned on.

Worried I might step on Wolfgang or one of the others, I use my phone as additional illumination.

"What's with the high beams?" Calliope grumbles sleepily.

I make the mistake of looking her way and spot a delicate shoulder sticking out of the covers. All the hard work in the cold shower is undone in an instant, the monster erection returning with a vengeance.

"You're in the middle," I point out, my voice a bit too husky. "If we're sharing the bed, you'll have to pick a side."

Even her disgruntled huff is sexy as she moves to the right side of the bed.

I get in from the left, staying as close to the edge as possible.

All right. If I want to put Tugev in his place, I had better fall asleep, and quickly.

Easier said than done. Knowing that Calliope is here, within my reach, is driving my libido insane.

Fuck. According to the nightstand clock, I've been tossing and turning for an hour, with nothing to show for it.

Has my dick been hard this whole time, or does it only stiffen when I pay attention to it? It is up and ready now. At the end of Viagra commercials, they warn you to seek medical help if you have a boner that lasts more than four hours, so I've got to be careful.

Maybe counting will help me forget how blue my balls are?

Nope. When I get to the number eight, I end up picturing the digit lying on its side, and the visual reminds me of Calliope's sweet ass. Pushing through anyway, I officially give up on number sixty-nine.

Counting is just too sexy of an activity.

I need to think of something else. Sometimes I imagine the way a game will play out in my head as a hybrid between guided imagery and mental practice. So I do this, and it goes well at first, but then I picture Calliope's reactions and the various mascot shenanigans she'd pull on me, and I become more alert... and, weirdly, even harder.

Fucking hell. Maybe I should attempt that progressive muscle relaxation technique the sport psychologist taught the whole team as a way to deal with stress. At the time, I thought they were all pansies for listening to the lecture intently, but hey, desperate times call for desperate measures.

Trying to remember how to do it, I flex my biceps and triceps, then let them relax.

Hmm. It feels nice, so I do the same with my other muscles, and get sleepier and sleepier until around the time I relax my glutes—which is when a dainty hand lands on my now-relaxed ass.

What the fuck?

I'm wide awake again, but Calliope's breathing is slow and even.

She's copping a feel in her sleep.

Fuck me.

This time around, progressive muscle relaxation doesn't help, so I practice another technique that was taught to us by that same shrink: deep breathing. I inhale air all the way down to my throbbing dick, then exhale it slowly. My next breath is slower and deeper, and the one after that even more so.

Eventually, I start to drift off—and of course, this is when Calliope drapes herself over me, like the world's sexiest scarf.

I freeze, not daring to move. She smells so fucking good. And she's so warm and soft. And is that a plump breast pushing against my side?

Oh, fuck. I'm going to blow if I don't move away this very second.

But I don't move.

I can't.

I should.

Fuck, I really need to.

I drag in a breath, gather all my willpower, and gently extricate myself from underneath her sleeping, soft, feminine form.

Panting like I've just skated around the rink fifty times, I flop onto my back and attempt to restart the deep breathing exercises. I throw in muscle relaxation as well and visualize myself winning tomorrow's game.

I don't know how much time passes or which technique works, but finally, I go under.

———

"Hey," says a sensual voice inside my dream. "You're on top of me."

I open my eyes to the dimly lit room.

Fuck.

On top of her is maybe an exaggeration, but I am spooning her, with my arm wrapped around her body, my palm cupping her soft breast, and my very hard dick pressed against the perfection that is her ass.

Gritting my teeth, I pull away. "I didn't wake you when *you* draped yourself all over me."

She rolls over to face me, eyes glinting. "I did no such thing."

"You also touched my ass," I growl. "And I didn't wake you up at that point either."

"Touched your ass?" She scoffs. "In your dreams."

Wet dreams, for sure. Fuck. I can't think in that direction. "Can I get some sleep now? I've got a big game tomorrow."

"I'm a mascot at that same game."

It's my turn to scoff. "Sure. Those are equally demanding jobs."

She scoots closer and jabs a finger in my face. "My job is just as important as yours."

I grab her wrist before she can poke my eyes out— depth perception is pretty important in hockey. "Calm down."

"Calm down?" she shouts. "You're unbearable."

A bear reference after I told her why they bother me so much?

I see white.

And red.

And pink.

Specifically, pink, plump lips speaking words that I no longer hear.

Drawn by a force more potent than gravity, I lean in and shut her up with a kiss.

CHAPTER 14
CALLIOPE

Why am I returning his kiss? I should push him away, but my hands draw him so close that I feel his chest hair tickle my naked collarbone, and it turns me on beyond any logic or reason.

As if picking up on my vibes, his kiss becomes deeper, rougher, and his tongue penetrates my mouth exactly the way I want his cock to—

Oh, yeah.

He rips off my pajama tank as if it were made of tissue paper, then captures my right breast with his callused hand as something big and hard presses against my belly through his boxers.

Very big and hard.

My mouth literally waters.

Panting, I wriggle out of my pajama shorts and underwear, then snake my hand into his boxers.

Because I have to feel it. I may die if I don't.

He groans as my fingers brush against his cock.

And I almost groan too because it feels like silk and steel, all hard and ready and so, so thick. So utterly magnificent.

"I want it inside me," I gasp, wrapping my hand around it just as he groans again and swoops in for another all-consuming kiss.

Lips locked to mine, he splays me on my back and gets on top of me.

Yes! I feel his boxers sliding down.

"Finally," I moan into his mouth before I guide his cock into me, luxuriating in the blissful stretch as his head pushes in.

He releases my lips to grunt in pleasure, then slowly thrusts deeper, allowing my body to adjust to the invasion.

"You're so soft," he growls. "And so wet for me."

I barely hold back another moan. "And you're hard. And—"

He suddenly stiffens, his eyes going wild. "Condom. I completely forgot."

I grab his ass because I'm going to die if he pulls out. "I'm clean and on the pill."

"Oh, good. Me too." His cock gets even harder inside me. "Clean, that is."

"Then stop getting distracted," I pant and pull him toward me, getting that cock so deep it hits a bundle of nerves I didn't even know I had.

My eyes roll into the back of my head.

He thrusts into me faster and faster, hitting that same spot.

Oh, my God. Toes curling, I come with a scream.

"Good, *ptichka*." His voice is a low rumble in my ear. "Give me another one."

Another one?

He pistons into me harder as he slides his hand down to my sensitive-from-orgasm clit and presses on just the right spot.

I cry out as a new tension crests inside me. "Michael! Oh, fuck, Michael…"

When the orgasm lands, it's so powerful I see white behind my closed eyelids and feel ecstasy streaking through every nerve ending. It feels like the pleasure tears me apart and then puts me back together again, but I'm changed in some ineffable way.

Michael groans as my muscles spasm around his cock, and I feel the hot jet of his release inside me. Another mini-orgasm blasts through me, causing me to space out for a second. Or several minutes. My sense of time is as fuzzy as Mr. Bloom right now.

Distantly, I feel Michael pull out and step away. He returns a moment later and cleans me up with a warm, wet washcloth. At least I think that's what he does. I'm too drained of energy to be sure. I'm just glad I'm on my back already because I can't move a muscle now.

Yawning like a contented rat, I let myself drift into sweet sleep.

———

I wake up to an angry growl that I will not compare to that of an angry bear because a promise is a promise.

Opening one eye, I see that Michael's ire is directed at the clock on the nightstand, of all things.

"Something wrong?" I reluctantly open my other eye.

"It's eleven-thirty." His tone is grim.

Oh. "But the game is at twelve," I say reassuringly. "We're not that far. I think we'll make it if we hurry."

He turns the angry gaze from the clock to me. "My routine is fucked."

"Routine?"

"A healthy breakfast and then a pre-game snack. Hydration. Warm-up. Taping sticks." He leaps from the bed, gloriously naked. "There's no time to give you the whole list." He hurries into the bathroom.

Shit. Whoever came up with the phrase "rude awakening" probably had Michael in mind. Everything he's just said implies that his getting up so late is somehow my fault, when in reality, he's the one who didn't let *me* sleep.

Even when I slept, I had crazy wet dreams.

Unless... Oh. I'm sore.

That very vivid dream involving the best sex of my life either happened for real, or I'm still asleep.

Michael and I need to talk. Pronto.

I leap to my feet, throw on a robe, and rush to the bathroom door.

It's locked.

I knock furiously.

"Give me a fucking minute!" Michael roars from the inside.

Shit. I also have a job to do at the game.

Grabbing my suitcase, I yank out the vacuum-sealed mascot suit and pull on the leggings and sports bra I'm going to wear underneath. Then I take out the food for my rats and allow them to have a feast.

Michael is still not out.

I exchange a worried glance with Wolfgang.

Meine Liebe, if you want anyone's cooperation, you have to weaponize that slice of cheddar.

"No," I tell Wolfgang. "The cheddar is for later, a treat for your performance on the ice."

I'm pretty sure Wolfgang understood that because his eyes glint with anticipation.

Striding to the bathroom door, I bang on it with all my might.

"One second," Michael snarls.

"I'm also running low on time!" I shout. "I won't even have time to put on my outfit if you don't come out."

"So put it on now," says a growl from inside the bathroom.

"I'll look ridiculous on the way to the stadium."

"Not my problem. Should've thought about that before oversleeping."

Fine. This won't even be the first time I'm furry in public. Also, he's fake-dating me and will have to walk in with me, so we'll both look ridiculous.

Sighing, I unseal Mr. Bloom and get inside him—but save the headgear for after I brush my teeth because priorities.

Finally, the door opens, and Michael steps out.

As I take him in, all angry words die on my lips.

Somehow, he's gotten more handsome overnight, though it's possible that my perception has been altered by those orgasms he gave me. And his shoulders have gotten broader. Even his eyes look blacker, and the white in them whiter.

Wait a second. The skin around his eyes has never looked this smoky before, and I can't believe that even the best orgasms would make me see *that*. It's exactly as if—

"Are you wearing black eye makeup?" And how is it that said makeup makes him *more* masculine?

"It's not fucking makeup," he growls. "It's war paint."

Not bothering to ask him what the difference is, I ask, "Isn't that cultural appropriation?" Unless... did ancient Russians wear war paint?

Michael narrows his eyes, and the war paint makes him look feral as a result. "Batman does this. Why can't I?"

Batman? Oh, right. The Dark Knight had to wear similar eye makeup to cover the white skin around his eyes while he wore his cowl. But... "What for?"

He takes a menacing step toward me. "The best game I ever played was after a fight where I got two black eyes. Now when it really matters, I do this to help my chances."

Overwhelmed by his nearness—and bigness—I step out of his way. "So you wouldn't let me into the bathroom because you were too busy with a silly superstition?"

His reply sounds exactly like the roar of a certain

wild animal that I promised not to compare him to. "I'm late." With that, he strides for the suite door.

"Wait!" I shout.

"What?" he barks over his shoulder.

"We need to talk." I dart a glance toward the bed. "About what happened."

"We shouldn't have done what we did," he says bluntly and steps out of the room.

I fight the urge to run after him and yell about just how much I agree that what we did was a mistake. But I can't. If I want to make it to the stadium, I need to hustle.

Fuming, I brush my teeth. Then, just to make things worse, stupid nature makes a call, so I have to take off my suit to take care of it.

As soon as I'm back inside Mr. Bloom, and Wolfgang is perched on my shoulder, I give my mirror self a quick pep talk, then take the bear's head and stomp into the hotel corridor.

As I approach the elevator, I see a cheesecake awaiting pickup from housekeeping, one that is missing only a single slice.

"It would be a shame to let food go to waste like this," I say to Wolfgang.

Meine Liebe, a cake made of cheese sounds like mana from the heavens.

"You can't have this. Sorry." I press the elevator button, put on my headgear, and grab the cake. "According to research, sugar is more addictive to a rat's brain than cocaine."

Wolfgang chirps.

Meine Liebe, now I have a craving for a cake made out of cocaine and cheese.

The elevator opens and the elderly couple inside examines my outfit and rat with barely suppressed smiles. In the hotel lobby, some people even chuckle, but when I get outside, no one seems to bat an eye. Everyone acts like clown bears carrying cheesecake with rats on their shoulders are as normal in New York as sky-high rent.

Once I get to the stadium, the security let me through without so much as a blink.

Interesting. I guess if I were a crazed fan who wanted to get into the game without a ticket, all I'd have to do is get myself a mascot suit.

Spotting a big clock, I put a steadying hand on Wolfgang and start running, pushing aside the hockey fans in my way, all to everyone's amusement.

"Hey," Coach says when he spots me. "Your custom skates are finished." He gestures across the hall. "They're on the bench in there."

I walk into the room in question with widening eyes. It's a locker room for women. Who knew such a beast existed in the world of hockey?

Because I'm in a rush, I set down the cake and quickly slide my feet into the skates. They fit snugly and perfectly, just like Michael's cock in my pussy.

Even when I come out, my cheeks still burn, so I'm glad for the bear's head that hides them from Coach's view.

"Let's hurry," he says when I come out with the cake. "You're on."

He leads me to the rink, and I'm grateful for all my earlier practice because seeing so many people in the stands is unnerving, to say the least.

"Hold this." I give Coach the cake. "It's for later." More specifically, for when I see Michael.

Gliding out onto the ice, I ignore my hammering heart as I start my shtick with the mascot dance.

CHAPTER 15
MICHAEL

By the time I'm finished gearing up, all my teammates are long done, and Coach is waiting to give a speech.

"Do you mind if I say a few words this time?" I ask him.

He looks taken aback but shakes his head.

"Listen, guys." I make eye contact with each and every one of them. "I know technically this game doesn't count toward anything, but I'm here to tell you that it does. It's actually the most important game of your life because everyone expects you to fail, and fuck that."

I continue with a speech that was strongly inspired by one that the US hockey team received during the 1980 Olympics, before they defeated the much stronger Soviet hockey team in a victory so unlikely it is known as the "Miracle on Ice."

Because we need our own miracle here.

When I finish, everyone cheers and not sarcastically, as far as I can tell.

"I don't think I'm going to give a speech today," Coach says with a grin. "Michael is a hard act to follow."

Isaac looks like I've pissed into his beer. He probably had a plan to play at captain and say a few words.

Everyone else cheers again, and we head to the rink.

On the way, I try to psych myself up the way I did my teammates, but that's difficult to do. Everything has gone so wrong up until now. For fuck's sake, I even broke my cardinal rule: no sex before a game. And what's worse, a part of me feels that even if we lose, having been inside Calliope might've been worth it.

Regardless, we shouldn't have done that before a game.

Not to mention, it was just too good. Scarily good.

"Man, are you seeing this?" Isaac asks, pointing toward the middle of the rink, bringing me back to reality.

I follow his finger, and my hands ball into tight fists.

The Yetis' team mascot—a red-eyed ape-like creature with white fur—slaps the face of the bear-suit that houses Calliope.

The world turns into a red tunnel of fury. Leaping for the rink, I close the distance between me and the yeti asshole with a couple of strides, and then my fist slams into the ape-like face hard enough that I feel a jaw under all that plush material.

Flailing extra-long furry arms, the yeti glides back until it hits a wall and collapses.

People in the stands laugh, probably thinking this is part of the mascot act.

"What the hell?" Calliope demands, her bear paws on the wide hips of her outfit. "Why did you do that?"

"I saw him slap you." I skate over to the fallen yeti and use the front of my blade to poke where the ass would be in a human. "Get up. I'm not done with you."

I would address the asshole by his name, but for the life of me, I can't recall what it is—that is, if it's still the same person as when I was on the team.

"It was just a skit," Calliope hisses. "He approached me when I was doing some photobombing and suggested we play-fight each other."

"Fuck." I feel like more of an ape than the guy I just punched. I bend a knee next to the yeti. "You all right?"

"Please," he says in a raspy voice. "Don't hit me again."

"He won't," Calliope says reassuringly.

"It was a misunderstanding," I say gruffly. "Sorry."

The yeti sits up. "It's okay. I guess. Help me up? The show must go on."

I help him up, and then Calliope makes me fall over an invisible rope as revenge. When my ass hits the ice, the crowd laughs uproariously.

After I get up, Calliope and the yeti approach me on opposite sides, and because her hand is hidden behind her back, I'm able to anticipate the moment when she throws a cake at my face—so I dodge it.

The cake slams into the face of the poor yeti—and he collapses yet again.

"Why did you do that?" Calliope demands angrily.

"I never agreed that you could pie me whenever you wanted."

I go help the guy get to his feet, again, but he tells me that he is fine, and that he fell just for laughs.

"That was a cheesecake, not a pie," Calliope retorts. "And you deserved to get hit with it."

"Agree to disagree." I turn to the other mascot. "I'll buy you a beer after the game."

"No, thank you," the ape says.

"Translation," Calliope says. "He never wants to see you again."

A hand lands on my shoulder. "The game is about to start," Isaac says.

"Sorry," I say again to the yeti and rejoin my teammates.

"Good job defending your lady's honor," Dante says from under his goalie's mask.

"I was simply in the mood to punch someone pale," I growl back at him. "So I'd be quiet if I were you."

"Whatever," Dante says, his tone more serious as he looks over the opposing team. "Where's Tugev?"

I scan my former teammates but do not spot the man in question. "Weird. I don't see him either."

"It's fine," Dante says. "I've seen him on video. Plus, he'll be at the face-off."

Right. Speaking of that.

"It's time." I skate over to the middle of the rink, where a referee is already waiting.

But then Noah Brown—a Canadian player who I thought was on a completely different team—skates over for the face-off.

"Where's Tugev?" I ask and then realize this is the first time I've spoken during a face-off in my life.

"Tugev retired," Noah says. "You didn't hear?"

I'm so stunned that I would miss the puck if the referee were to let go of it right now. Then a wave of righteous fury overtakes me, one that was already primed when I thought Calliope was under attack.

How dare Tugev not be at this game? The whole point was that—

The puck hits the ice.

My instincts kick in. I take it from Noah and pass it to Jack, as was part of the plan.

Channeling all my frustration with Tugev into skating, I quickly end up face to mask with Jason, a.k.a. Friday, the Yetis' goalie, and as per the plan, the puck is passed back to me.

Jason looks ready, but I don't give a shit. I feign a shot, then smash the puck and score right between Jason's legs.

My team goes wild, and the jumbotron shows both Calliope and the rat on her shoulder clapping their paws.

CHAPTER 16
CALLIOPE

Until today, I've been pretty lukewarm on hockey, especially for a team mascot. I still don't know the difference between a wrist or snap shot, for example, or why the players get a five-minute timeout for the kind of fighting that would mean assault charges outside the rink. And yet, I watch in awed fascination as Michael and the rest of the Florida Bears fiercely battle their much stronger opponent.

Michael, in particular, is magnificent, especially when he scores a goal.

I almost forget that I'm mad at him for saying that sleeping with me was a mistake. What's worse, watching him makes me want to repeat said mistake again. Which is insane. It's bad enough our fake dating feels real on some occasions. If I have any more orgasms like the ones he gave me last night, the line between—

The sound of a horn announces the end of the game,

and the score is 3 for the Yetis and 4 for the Florida Bears.

As in, we won!

The whole team piles up on top of Michael in jubilation. When all the manly emotions settle down, I skate over to him and take off my bear mask.

"We did it!" he shouts, then leans down to give me a passionate kiss.

Oh, my. The noises around us grow faint, and I lose track of time. It's not until Michael pulls away that I see us on the kiss cam and realize that this was only for appearances' sake.

Something inside me contracts, but I do my best to shake off the bizarre disappointment. "Congratulations." I touch my lips. "I know you wanted this win."

His excitement visibly wanes. "What I wanted was to best Tugev, but the bastard retired before I got the chance."

Huh. "Isn't he the team owner?"

Michael nods.

"You beat his team. I'm sure he's not thrilled about that."

"Not the same," he says grimly.

Coach skates over with an ecstatic expression. "That was amazing teamwork. Outstanding job! I always knew you had it in you." He pats Michael on the shoulder.

He's right. It *was* good teamwork, which must have been as natural a behavior for my boo as yoga is for a bear.

Michael nods gruffly. "I couldn't have done it without your coaching."

Coach waves that away and winks at me. "How about our new mascot?" he asks. "You sure she wasn't an inspiration as well?"

"Sure." Michael slants me a glance. "She made me realize that getting my teammates to play better hockey shouldn't be more difficult than teaching a rat to ride a unicycle."

"This win will help at the fundraiser tonight," Coach says.

Michael's expression darkens. "I mentioned that to you in confidence."

"What fundraiser?" I ask.

Coach turns to Michael with an expression of exaggerated shock. "You didn't invite Calliope?"

"No," Michael growls. "I thought about it, but—"

"Why do you need to go to a fundraiser?" I ask. "Is it for your secret project?"

That's the only reason I can think of for him not wanting to involve me. Or the only reason that doesn't hurt my feelings. Unless he's planning on bringing someone else? Someone who wears small skates? No. He wouldn't risk ruining our ploy and being spotted by the paparazzi. Even so, just the idea of it makes me sick.

"Yes." Michael looks furtively at the people leaving the stands. "I need to raise some money… and I *could* use your help."

"*My* help?" I glance at Wolfgang as though he might understand this better.

Meine Liebe, say "yes." Fundraisers mean hors d'oeuvres, and that means lots and lots of delicious parmesan.

"I'm not great at socializing," Michael says, understating the case by a mile. "If you came, I think things would go smoother."

Huh. That's oddly nice of him to say. "Is it a swanky event?" I ask.

He nods.

I bite my lip. "I have nothing to wear."

"I'll get you whatever you need." His eyes glint with such heat I can tell that whatever clothes he's just pictured wouldn't cover much of my skin.

Said skin heats up at the thought, but I keep my face neutral. "In that case, let's make a deal," I say sweetly. "You tell me what the project is, and I'll be your escort."

My latest guess: he wants to take DNA from inside the bellies of ancient stuck-in-amber mosquitoes and use that to resurrect an extinct species of saber-toothed panda.

Michael and Coach exchange glances.

"I thought you already explained it to her when you gave her those skates," Coach says.

The suspiciously small and feminine skates I was just thinking about. Ones that made me think a woman might be involved. But I don't see the connection to some secret project. Unless... do pandas prefer women to men?

"Fine," Michael growls. "But this is to be a private matter between us."

Like the fact that we slept together? "Sure."

He scans the people who are still in the process of

leaving the stadium. "Let's go back to our hotel room, and I'll tell you there. Then we'll go shopping."

"Okay," I say, though my curiosity is at lethal levels now. "I'll see you there."

———

As soon as I arrive back at our honeymoon suite, I jump into the shower to wash the unladylike bear-suit sweat from under my arms. Then I work on my hair and makeup until there's a knock on the bathroom door.

"One second." I pull on a robe and come out, only to bump into Michael.

Fuck me. His hair is tousled, and he smells freshly showered—which means he must've done it in the locker room.

"When are we going shopping?" he asks, his face unreadable.

"Not so fast. You promised to tell me."

Sighing, he walks over to the dining area and takes a seat. "Can we at least talk while waiting for room service? I'm starving."

"Fine." I call and order for everyone, including my rat crew. Then I look at Michael. "Now… we need to talk."

His gaze strays to the bed. "About a number of things."

Shit. I think I'm blushing. "We don't need to talk about what happened *there*. You said it was a mistake, and I don't disagree."

At least my brain doesn't. My other organs, especially my vagina and heart, aren't so sure.

"I said we shouldn't have done what we did *before the game*," he says. "But hey, we won, so I guess—"

"Nice try. I'm pretty sure you meant 'mistake' in a broader sense. And you were right."

He grits his teeth. "And why was it such a mistake?"

"Because we're not really dating, and I don't do casual hookups." And it would be pointless for us to date for real because that would only last until he met my family.

"We also work together," he says. "And you hate my guts."

"No, you hate *my* guts," I counter.

"No, you—"

There's a knock on the door, and it turns out to be room service.

I feed the rats first, and as usual, Lenin asks for seconds, and then thirds.

Tovarisch, we the proletari-rat do all the hard work, which naturally increases the appetite.

"Fine." I give him a whole baby carrot, and that seems to pacify him, at least for the moment.

Getting back to the table where my tacos are waiting for me, I smile at the speed with which Michael wolfs down most of the quinoa and salmon that he ordered.

"So," I say after he also downs a whole glass of tomato juice in one gulp. "What's the secret project?"

"Right." He looks thoughtful as he devours the rest of his meal. "The project is meant to give others the lucky break that I got."

He looks to be finished with his explanation, but I have no clue what he means, and I tell him so.

He sighs. "I want to give kids in orphanages a chance to play hockey—or other sports—and thus set them on a path to a better life."

My head spins. Of all the possibilities, this is not something I expected—and not just because this has nothing to do with pandas. This is a genuinely kind-hearted thing to do, and that word combination isn't something that pops into my head when I think of Michael.

Realizing he's looking at me expectantly, I say, "Wow. That is amazing. How is it going?"

"Not great. So far, I've only been able to help local Florida kids, and even that is mostly thanks to Coach. He was the one who got the league higher-ups to allow my kids access to the rink and old equipment. Whatever they've needed beyond that, I've purchased with my own money—and that of a few sponsors that I've found thus far."

Oh. So those small skates he gave me were meant for kids, not women? The relief I feel is pretty ridiculous and should be blamed on how sexy Michael is when he eats. And breathes.

"Anyway," he continues. "I want to drastically scale up what I've done so far. It needs to be a real foundation that can help children from all over the world, but that requires some serious money, which is why I've been reaching out to people who I thought might be able to help."

"I'll help in any way I can." I glance at my rats as an

idea forms in my mind. "If you'd like, I can bring my little troupe and set up a show at the fundraiser, to draw a crowd. Once people stop by, we can tell them about your foundation."

His eyes light up. "You'd do that?"

"Sure." I'm always glad for an excuse to put on a performance.

"That would be great," he says. "It solves my biggest problem: walking up to people I don't know. This way, they'll come to me."

I smile. "Please don't look so grateful. There could be people there who aren't fans of rats."

"Not fans of rats?" His expression is mock-horrified. "They must be dead inside. Such heartless people wouldn't have donated to my cause anyway, so filtering them out will save time when it comes to pitching."

"It's settled then." I put the last bite of taco into my mouth. "Now let's go shopping."

CHAPTER 17
MICHAEL

"This one?" Calliope dangles a strapless black cocktail dress in front of her body. "Or this?" She replaces the black with a red one, which seems to be even shorter and with more fabric missing in the back.

My nostrils flare. Picturing her in either outfit makes me hard, which in turn makes it difficult to make decisions. "Why don't you try them on?"

Shit. I've essentially asked for a private strip show, so I fully expect her to tell me to go to the dick.

"That's a great idea." She runs to the dressing room, picking up a few more dresses on the way.

As I wait, I surreptitiously position my legs so that my hard-on is not so noticeable—and I'm glad that I do because when she comes out wearing that short black dress, my dick needs all the extra space, and then some.

Hell, even Wolfgang—whom she's left next to me— seems to whistle.

And that's before she twirls, giving me a view of her lithe back and the perfection that is her ass.

"What do you think?" she asks shyly.

"You look magnificent, *ptichka*," I say, the words coming out husky. "You'll draw a crowd without the need for a rat show." And I'll punch them all in the face.

Her cheeks turn pink. "Thanks. Should I just take this one?"

"No," I say, much too eagerly. "Let's see the others." Even if that means my balls might actually explode into blue dust.

The red dress exposes even more of her milky skin, and I find myself mumbling the compliment because my dick has left no blood flow for my tongue to properly operate.

Things only get worse from there. Or better, depending on how I look at it. The white dress is shorter than the others. The shiny silvery one pushes her boobs up.

"Which is your favorite?" she asks.

"It's hard to choose." I want to get them all, but not for the fundraiser. My new fantasy is to have her wear each of those for me, very privately, in my bedroom. "You make them all look amazing."

Picking just one is like picking which of my balls is my favorite.

"But if you had to pick a favorite?" She dangles two dresses in her hands expectantly.

"Red?" It's no doubt the color her commie rat named Lenin would choose, if he were here.

She frowns. "I think I like black more."

I arch an eyebrow. "Black looks amazing on you. As I said, they all do."

"Yes, but you like red more." She waves at the saleswoman. "I think I should try on a few more dresses."

And boy, does she try on more. If my spank bank were a real bank, it would need to open a few new branches at this point.

Could she be teasing me? Is this an attempt at seduction?

If it's the latter, she succeeded on dress number one. At this point, I can't even recall why it would be a bad idea to fuck her brains out—especially seeing how I don't have a game tomorrow, or anytime soon.

No. I think it's my dick's wishful thinking that is making me think this is a seduction. She—

"What about now?" Calliope asks. "Do you have a favorite?"

This is starting to sound like a trick question. "Can I see the black again?"

Nodding approvingly, she disappears into the changing room, and I wait with bated breath and a hard dick.

When she comes out, I look at the dress as if for the first time. "This is the one," I say solemnly. And by that, I mean when I picture her in my mind from now on, she'll either be wearing this dress or, more likely, nothing at all.

She beams at me. "Who knew you had such good taste?"

———

By the time we return to the hotel room, all I have time for is a cold shower and a quick change into my suit. Then, per Calliope's instructions, I knock before leaving the bathroom, "in case she's not decent."

Fuck. Thinking of what that could entail undoes all the benefits of the cold shower.

"Come out," she says.

When I step into the suite, she's turned away from the giant mirror, thanks to which I can see her from the front and back.

"Wow," I say in an understatement of the century.

Her cheeks redden. "You saw me like this at the store."

Should I tell her I could see her in that dress a million more times and still have the same over-reaction?

"You didn't have your hair done at the store," I say lamely. "It adds to the 'wow.'" And she has put her hair in an updo, which exposes her long, delicate, and very kissable neck.

She beams at me. "You don't look too bad yourself, boo." She walks over and grabs my tie. "Let me just adjust that."

As she fixes the wayward tie, I fight the over-whelming urge to rip her dress off and carry her to the giant bed.

"That's better." She bats her eyelashes at me prettily. "Now we can go."

Leaving is the last thing I want to do, but we're late as is. Plus, she wouldn't want me to take her to bed. She's not into casual hookups, and I'm not sure if we have the time to start a real relationship. Not that the latter is a good idea. If we dated for real, just as I'd start to care about her, she'd leave, just like everyone else in my life. No, it's better—

"Here." She thrusts the rat carrier into my hand. "Make yourself useful."

She then rummages through her suitcase and takes out some hoops "for the rats to jump through," balls "for the rats to balance on," a unicycle for obvious reasons, a tiny soccer ball, and two goalposts.

"Shouldn't that be a puck?" I point at the soccer ball.

She shrugs. "I taught them to play soccer before I knew I'd have a hockey career." She stashes all the trick accessories into a bag and swaps it for the carrier in my hands. "Let's go."

———

"So," I say while we sit next to each other in an Uber. "You didn't know you'd have a hockey career?"

She shakes her head. "I worked as a character in theme parks, but then I got blacklisted from that field, so I took the mascot gig. What I really want, though, is to do rat shows for a living."

"You do?" I glance at the rat carrier. "Why?"

She thinks about my question for a block or so. "Historically, rats have had bad PR and have been blamed for things like spreading the plague."

"Is it bad PR?" I ask. "I thought they really *did* spread the plague."

She shakes her head. "Recent studies have debunked that theory. It was humans who spread it, not rats."

I give Wolfgang an apologetic nod. "I didn't realize."

"Few people do. The reality is, rats are cute and intelligent creatures. When it comes to cohabitation with people, they are superior to cats in every way, yet the bad PR is making it so they are not nearly as mainstream as felines. Worse still, people create things such as rat traps and rat poison—which are terrible."

I nod. "Your shows are meant to cast rats in a more positive light?"

"Exactly. My goal is to help the great work that Pixar started with *Ratatouille*. Work that was continued by rodent heroes such as the Pizza Rat."

I glance at the streets of New York outside, half expecting to see a rat carrying a slice of pizza as we speak. "I think I get it."

Hell, I myself have been on the other end of bad PR —though, granted, it might actually have been deserved in my case.

"So," I say. "If you did have a show, what would the rats be doing?"

For the rest of our trip, she tells me in minute detail, and I realize something I never would have imagined.

I'd like to see this rat show of hers.

———

The fundraiser is the kind of fancy that is only possible in New York. If it had a theme, it would be "old money" and/or "snobbery." Most of the women wear pearls that they seem very eager to clutch, and the men all have a rare-for-hockey combo of soft hands and never-been-broken noses.

Just thinking about striking up a conversation with any of these people causes my blood pressure to spike way more than it would if I had to step into a boxing ring with a heavyweight champion.

"Let's set up here." Calliope gestures at one of the long tables in the middle of the room.

"Sure."

Glad to have an excuse to postpone having to shmooze, I carry the bag with rat paraphernalia over to the table and watch as Calliope sets it all up.

"Now I'll do my thing, and people will hopefully come over," she says.

At her urging, the rats play soccer—an activity chosen because it's a sport and therefore should allow me to segue into mentioning my foundation.

A couple of people gather and watch in fascination until the performance is finished, with Marco—or maybe Polo—scoring the last goal.

"That was amazing," says one of the men, turning to his wife. "Wasn't it, Sugar?"

I open my mouth to somehow talk about the fundraiser, but Sugar butts in, asking if Calliope has a business card.

"No," Calliope replies. "Sorry. This isn't about me."

She nods my way. "The performance was a means to draw attention to Michael's foundation."

Everyone turns my way, so I launch into the speech I've rehearsed so often in my head. To my shock, not only are they interested, a few even pull out their checkbooks—including Sugar's husband.

"Now that that's settled," Sugar says, turning to Calliope, "how do I reach you in case I want to hire you to put on a show like that for me?"

Using nearby napkins, Calliope writes down her number.

"Thanks," Sugar says and departs.

"Damn," I say. "You might just get your show sooner than you thought."

Calliope shakes her head. "I want to be performing in theaters or circuses. Sugar clearly has a private event, like a birthday, in mind."

"Still. She might have a guest at her event who owns a theater or a circus."

"How about we focus on you for now?" Calliope sets up the soccer game again, and it draws an even bigger crowd.

"Are you Honey and Boo Boo?" asks a lady when the performance is over.

"Yes," Calliope says. "Though we don't go by those nicknames."

Knowing that we are celebrities opens up people's checkbooks even quicker, and on top of that, Calliope gives away two more napkins with her number.

Around the time we gather a third crowd, a person walks over that makes me do a double take.

He is someone I expected to see earlier today.

"Tugev," I grit out. "What are you doing here?"

He and his date look up from the rats, and he acts as though he's seeing me for the first time.

"Mi... Medvedev?" he says, eyes widening.

My jaw twitches. I know he was initially going to say "Misha" but decided not to spew an insult that would undoubtedly cause a scene.

"What are you doing here?" he asks.

"I asked first." I cross my arms in front of my chest. "And since we're throwing questions around, why weren't you at the game?"

"I brought him here," says his date with a grin. She then extends her slender hand to me. "Hi, I'm Sophia. You must know Mason from hockey."

"Call me Michael." I shake her hand. "Did you also forbid him from playing earlier?"

"I didn't play because I'm retired," Tugev growls.

So that's true? "How convenient. Just as I was going to kick your ass on the ice, you retire."

"Oh, please," he says with derision. "Had I been there, you and your team would have lost."

"What he means is 'congratulations on your win,'" Sophia says.

"I meant what I said," Tugev says to her. Turning my way, he grudgingly adds, "I was impressed with your teamwork. Or more specifically, that you managed any at all."

Is that a compliment or a diss?

In that moment, Lenin scores the last goal, and Calliope looks up from the rat game.

"Hey," she says, looking at Tugev. "Aren't you the guy Michael wanted to beat today?"

Tugev smirks. "I didn't realize he cared so much about me. I'm flattered."

I ball my hands into fists. "You wish. But you're going to get *flattened* if you keep—"

Calliope puts a calming hand on my shoulder. "Did you tell him about your foundation? With both of you being so much into hockey, he might just be the perfect sponsor."

"What foundation?" Sophia asks, looking genuinely intrigued.

Tugev doesn't say anything, but he raises an eyebrow very pointedly.

"Right." I grit my teeth, think of the kids, and go into my spiel. I even adjust for the audience, emphasizing that I'm interested in starting with hockey as the sport and Russia and former Soviet republics as the recruiting locations.

"That is amazing," Sophia says and elbows Tugev.

"I agree," he says. "Tell me more."

Shocked by this turn of events, I talk for a while. To his credit, Tugev asks some intelligent questions. Soon, he and Sophia recommend me their lawyer, suggest some people who could serve on the foundation board, and invite me to more events where I can raise funds.

"Have you spoken to Orehov about this?" Tugev asks toward the end.

"Why?"

Orehov is a strange hockey player because there are persistent rumors linking him to the Russian mob. I have no idea if said rumors are true, but the one time he fought someone on the ice, the guy disappeared afterward.

"They say he has a lot of connections in Russia," Tugev says. "Figure that might come in handy if you plan to help kids there."

"I think I can get by without him," I say. "I regularly get letters from Russian fans, so that's who I'd ask for help." Because the last thing I want is to mix helping children with even a hint of the Russian mob.

"Whatever works best for you." Tugev goes into his inner jacket pocket to pull out his checkbook. "This is just the start." He fills out the check and hands it to me.

When I see the number, my eyes widen. This is more money than anyone has ever contributed to my cause, even if you combine it all and add a few zeros. I guess this could've been expected. After all, Tugev is a billionaire, but—

The loud gasp from Calliope's mouth is weirdly sexy. She's also noticed the obscene number.

"This will help a lot of kids," I say solemnly, looking at Tugev. "Thank you, Mason."

He hands me a business card. "Like I said, that's just the beginning. Let's touch base when you've grown the fund a bit, and I could make a more meaningful contribution."

Stunned at the idea of an even bigger check, I nod and watch as he and Sophia leave to mingle with other people.

"Do you think he did that because he felt bad about missing the game?" Calliope asks.

I shrug. "If that's the case, I'm glad he retired. This money changes everything."

She squeezes my shoulder. "Let's keep going while the going is hot."

"Sure."

The rat show resumes, and we return to our fundraising mode—which somehow goes a lot smoother now that I have that giant check. It's like people can sense success and are attracted by it. That or I'm better at social skills when the pressure is off. In fact, I lose count of the checks I get, and then, just as the latest group leaves, a woman steps up to the podium in the front of the room and taps on the microphone.

"The dance-a-thon is about to begin," she says. "But we're short on dancers. Anyone want to volunteer?" She looks directly at us. "Particularly anyone who's a viral sensation?"

I shake my head.

Calliope does the same.

"Oh, don't be shy," the woman says. "I'm pretty sure we'll raise plenty of money if you participate—and it can go to the cause of your choice."

"Even if it's his?" Calliope points at me.

"Sure," the woman says.

Shit. Are we actually going to do this?

Probably not. Calliope still looks uncertain. "I can't leave my rats alone," she says.

"I'll watch them," the woman says, and she must have a lot of Botox because she manages to wrinkle her nose without causing any wrinkles.

"I'll make a pledge of a hundred grand if you do

dance," Sophia says, eyes glinting mischievously. "I'm sure other people will be even more generous." She nods at her date.

Other people get into the spirit of pressuring us and also make pledges. Then, according to the instigator woman, there turns out to be additional money coming from the hoi polloi who will be watching the dance-a-thon online.

"We should do it," Calliope whispers into my ear. "The kids could use that money."

"Tugev's check makes it so we don't need to do anything we don't want to do," I whisper back. "You've done so much already." I doubt I would've raised a fraction of this insane amount by myself.

Her lips brush softly against my ear as she whispers, "Dancing together would also help sell our charade. Real couples dance."

Fuck it. Pantomiming something a figure skater might do, I extend my hand theatrically. "Would you care to dance?"

Blushing for some unfathomable reason, she takes my hand, and we walk over to the dance floor, where we are joined by the volunteers that the lady mentioned earlier.

"How about you two?" said lady says to Tugev and Sophia. "Will you join?"

They do. So does another couple, and a few more after that.

As we wait for the music, I realize that my heart is hammering—and not just because of Calliope's proximity or the fact that her slender hand is enveloped in mine. Nor am I bothered by the fact that this perfor-mance is going to be streamed live. No. It's hammering due to a belated realization.

I want this fake relationship with my team's mascot to be real.

CHAPTER 18
CALLIOPE

"**O**ne More Time" by Daft Punk belts through the speakers all around us, and we begin moving, which gives me a flashback from when Michael was so recently inside me. Or maybe it's not just a flashback. Maybe I want him back there? All I know is I'm unnaturally turned-on in front of the richest people in New York, and Michael's powerful body gyrating next to me isn't helping in the slightest.

"You're a good dancer," he murmurs into my ear.

"It's all about balance and rhythm," I gasp into his. "And you're not bad yourself." And by that, I mean he's sex on a hockey stick.

Smirking, he moves his body even more sensually, while I pray my reaction to him stays inside my thong.

When the song stops, the dancers are scored, with the couple near us getting the highest marks.

Michael leans in and I half-expect him to kiss me, but he speaks softly into my ear instead. "This dance-a-thon is a chance to beat Tugev."

I frown. "Even after all that money he gave to the kids?"

He shrugs. "This is a competition. Someone has to win. Why not us?"

"I guess."

What do you call the female equivalent of blue balls? Blue vulva? Asking for a friend.

The next dance is even hotter, and we get the highest scores. Unfortunately, Sophia and Tugev score in the next round, and given the looks the two males exchange, Tugev is just as competitive as Michael.

"We need more sexiness points next round," Michael informs me.

"How?" And is it a good idea? I'm a few such points away from climbing Michael like a panda might the most delicious—and very hard—bamboo.

"Stay closer," he says. "And gyrate more."

"If I get any closer, we might need a condom," I mutter under my breath, but I do as he suggests, earning us another high score—and bringing myself ever closer to blue vulva.

Unfortunately, despite our best gyrations on the next song, Tugev and Sophia come out victorious—which means it's now a draw.

Up next is the Cha Cha—which, being a ballroom dance, requires prior practice that Michael and I don't have. Nor do Tugev and his date, it seems. Instead, the highest scores go to an adorable older couple who are so good they might just be retired pros. This same couple dominates the Waltz round that follows, and the Tango, and the rest of the ballroom dances—which makes them the winners of the whole competition. No one seems to care about who got second or third place.

The expression on Michael's face is thunderous, making me fear for the older couple's safety. To our left, Tugev wears a matching mien—which just confirms that all hockey players are too competitive to be considered sane.

"Let's go check on my rats," I say.

Michael seems to shake off the violent fantasies he was harboring against the winners. "Yeah. And then let's leave?"

I nod. The sooner we can get back to the hotel, the sooner I can change my panties.

———

When we reach the door of our honeymoon suite, I notice it's not fully closed, so I mention this to Michael.

"Let me see." He bends down to examine the lock, and every muscle in his body seems to tense.

"Someone broke in," he says grimly as he straightens. His hands ball into tight fists.

"You think?" I push on the door, and it opens.

The lock was clearly tampered with.

"Stay here," Michael orders. "I'm going in to—"

"No." I grab his elbow. "What if they're still there?"

There's a dark gleam in his eyes. "That's what I'm hoping for."

I tighten my grip on him. "No. I forbid it."

"You forbid it?" He frees his arm and narrows his eyes.

"You could get hurt." And just the thought of it fills my insides with liquid nitrogen.

"Your stalker is about to get hurt, not me." The chilling way he says the words reminds me of that terrifying mauling scene from *The Revenant*.

I gape at him. "You think this is related to—"

"Yes. I do."

I grab his arm again. "In that case, I *really* don't want you going in there. What if this psycho has a gun?"

He shrugs. "It would still not be a fair fight."

It's official. Testosterone is a toxin. "Please. Don't. I'm worried he'll get past you and then grab me."

"Oh." Michael turns my way, concern written all over his features. "I didn't think of that. Go downstairs. Now."

"No. We're going together."

He looks reluctant, so I add, "What if the stalker is in the lobby?"

"Right," he grits out. "Let's go."

We take the elevator together, sprint to the concierge, and explain the situation. Soon, two police officers appear, as well as a woman who seems to be upper management of this chain of hotels. The cops go up to the suite, but when they come back, they tell us no one was inside—and that the room didn't seem to have been ransacked.

"Except for the bear suit," says the cop with the beard. "Someone ripped that up."

My mascot suit? Why?

"You should go see if anything is missing," says the manager.

We agree, and she accompanies us alongside the police as we head upstairs. We find that everything is indeed in order, except for my suit, which someone has cut into teddy-bear-sized chunks.

"Who would do this?" I goggle at the poor suit.

"And why?" the manager asks.

"Some weird fan?" the bearded cop suggests.

"I think it's a stalker," Michael says. "Someone who's after Calliope." He glowers at the suit. "I think this was some sort of a sick ritual."

Wow. That's dark. Does he think whoever did this was picturing me inside the suit as he mangled it?

I turn to the woman. "Can you find out who this was based on security footage?"

She nods. "The officers have already requested it. Unfortunately, we recently switched to a new system, so I was told that it might take a few days to get a hold of the footage."

"You'll send it to me as soon as you have it," Michael says imperiously.

"I'm sending it to the police."

The expression on Michael's face causes both cops to lay their hands over their guns. "You will send the footage to me or—"

"Bear in mind, we'll be in Florida in a couple of days," I chime in. I have a feeling Michael is about to get himself arrested for making deadly threats or some such, so I quickly add, "And if this is a stalker situation, he might follow us home and leave nothing to do for the police in New York." What I don't mention is my skepticism about the cops even looking at the footage given nothing was stolen and no one was hurt.

"Actually," the bearded cop says, "if—"

"I've had enough of this," Michael growls. He looms over the manager. "Do you know who we are?"

She shakes her head.

"Google 'Honey and Boo Boo,'" he says grimly. "And then ask yourself if you want us to publicly shit all over your hotel, which is what will happen if you don't comply with my very reasonable request."

The woman takes her phone out, does a search, and pales.

"What's your email?" she asks Michael.

He gives it to her, and she promises she'll send the footage he wants.

"We're going to go," the bearded cop says.

"Thanks for your help," I say.

As soon as they leave, Michael asks the manager for another room.

"Make that two," I say.

Now that the game is over, they should have more availability.

"Two?" The manager looks confused. "Aren't you together?"

Shit. The fake relationship. "We had a fight." Hey, this isn't exactly a lie. "I need some space."

"One room." Michael turns my way, eyes squinty. "I insist."

"Why?" Despite the scare, or perhaps because of it, I'm the horniest I've ever been, and therefore can't trust myself to be in the same bed with him. Especially after yesterday.

He walks over and takes my hand. "Until this stalker thing is sorted, I don't want you to be alone."

Damn it. He makes sense—but this also means we'd share a space for at least a few more days, an idea that makes me feel weirdly bubbly.

"Okay," I say to the manager with my best poker face on. "A single room, please."

"You can have the Presidential Suite," she chirps. "It has two bedrooms, so you can choose to sleep in any arrangement that you desire."

Why am I so disappointed by the very idea of two bedrooms? Because I am, and as the manager helps us make the move to the Presidential Suite, Michael doesn't look pleased either.

"I'll hire private security to watch the hallway outside your door," the manager says before leaving. "And while we wait for them, I'll have a couple of porters do the job."

Wow. "Thank you. You've gone above and beyond." I can even almost forgive the two-room idea.

Almost.

"No problem," she says and exits.

"When did we fight?" Michael demands as soon as we are alone.

"What?"

"You told her we had a fight," he says. "What were you referring to?"

I blink at him. "I was just covering up for saying we need two rooms."

"Ah." He takes a step toward me. "But that leaves the question: why *do* you want two separate rooms?"

My heartbeat spikes. "Why not? That's what we wanted last night."

Those pitch-black eyes gleam dangerously. "That was *before*."

I lift my chin. "Before the act that you called a mistake?"

As his nostrils flare, I realize even his nose is strong and attractive.

"Pot, meet kettle," he grits out. "It was you who called what happened a mistake. Something about casual hookups and claims that I do not date."

"Well, you don't. You have some bullshit rule about it."

He closes the distance and lifts my chin with his bent knuckles. "There are always exceptions to every rule."

With that, he claims my lips in a vicious, all-encompassing kiss.

CHAPTER 19
MICHAEL

She returns my kiss with a ferocity I didn't expect, and then she reaches down to unbuckle my belt.

Some kind of beast—no doubt a bear—awakens inside me, and I fight the urge to roar as I pick her up and carry her to the giant bed.

In a frantic frenzy, we tug at each other's clothes until they are a pile on the edge of the bed, revealing Calliope in all her pale, delectable glory.

"I want to fuck you so bad." The words come out of me with a pained groan. "You have no idea what you do to me, *ptichka*."

In reply, her cheeks and breasts turn a deeper pink than her hair. "I bet I want to fuck you more."

"There's no way that can be true." I cup her breast.

"Does everything need to be a competition with you?" she gasps, her nipple pebbling under my fingers.

"No." I spread her legs and feather kisses from her

knee up to her thigh. "When it comes to you, I feel like I've already won."

"That doesn't even make sense," she says dazedly. "If—"

My kisses reach the damp, heated flesh of her pussy, and that seems to shut her up—a trick I'll keep in mind for future reference.

When I take a greedy lick of her entrance, she tastes intoxicatingly of cotton candy, roasted pecans, and something ineffable that is purely her.

A desperate moan escapes her lips, urging me on to lick higher, where her tightening clit shyly hides in a pink hoodie of flesh.

"Oh, my," she breathes as I reach my destination.

Gripping her by her deliciously round butt cheeks, I lift her toward me and circle my tongue around her little bud, making her moan again. And again.

"That's right," I murmur right into her pretty flesh as her muscles start to quiver. "Come for me."

She does, and with a scream.

I glide my tongue up her belly until I reach her neck, which I nibble. "That was only the beginning," I whisper sensuously into her ear. "Tonight, I will make you come more than you ever have in your life."

She shakes her head languidly. "Like I was saying, competitive."

Fuck. Maybe I am. Because I want to fuck her so thoroughly it will erase from her mind any memory of anyone but me.

"Turn over," I order hoarsely.

"Why?" she demands but obeys.

"You're getting a glute massage." And I'm finally getting a handful of that sweet ass that has been taunting my every waking moment.

"Okay." She lifts her butt in the air, no doubt in a misguided attempt to aid me.

Fuuuuck. The thought of a massage is gone from my mind. What I really want to do is slide my dick inside her, from behind, and pound into her until—

No.

If I'm to achieve my earlier objective, I'll have to exercise all of my available self-control.

Grabbing a handful of pale flesh, I squeeze with both my hands and then knead the muscle.

"Wow." She visibly relaxes. "That feels pretty nice."

Pretty nice? I intensify my ministrations until she turns to putty in my hands and moans in pleasure.

When my dick feels like it might just explode, I lick her from behind until she comes for me one more time, hands balling over the starchy sheets and a desperate cry escaping her lips.

"Turn over," I order gruffly.

She does, and I feel an inordinate amount of satisfaction when I see just how tight her nipples and hooded her eyes are.

She looks properly fucked, and my dick has been nowhere near her yet.

"Here." I bring the index and middle finger of my right hand over to her perfect lips. "Make these nice and wet."

Eyes widening, she sucks my fingers like a very good girl, and when I'm satisfied with the resulting lubrication, I glide them inside her, gently stretching— and nearly come myself as I feel the slick heat within her.

The expression of bliss on her face urges me on, and I slide my fingers in and out, then crook them, locating a bundle of tissue just behind—

"Yes!" she gasps. "There. Please."

Well, if she's going to beg so nicely, I don't have a choice, do I? I concentrate on the spot that I've found until her toes curl and she shouts as she reaches another orgasm.

"Good job, *ptichka*," I croon hoarsely. "Now one more."

"What?" Her eyes widen.

Since actions are better than words, I put my tongue on her clit again, and all it takes is a couple of licks before she comes undone for me again.

"Now," I growl. "I want to be inside you."

"Finally." She grabs a condom, rips it open, and sheaths my dick.

I don't know if I've just developed a new kink or what, but seeing those sparkly nails near my shaft almost makes me pop my load all too soon, but thankfully, I do not. Instead, I very carefully enter her incredibly snug pussy and let us both adjust to the sensations for a second before I dare to move.

"No," she pleads, wriggling underneath me. "Don't be gentle. I want it very hard."

Did I think I was beast-like earlier? Because that can't compare with the ferocity with which I thrust into her, all too glad to give her exactly what she wants.

"Yes!" she screams, raking her nails down my back. "Like that!"

I piston into her with everything I have, and she comes all over my cock, again and again, until I lose count of her orgasms along with my mind. Finally, with a savage grunt, my own release bursts forth.

The aftermath is a bit hazy in my mind. She leaves to wash up, and I think I do the same, but then we find ourselves locked in an embrace and under the covers, at which point I fall into the deepest, sweetest sleep of my life.

CHAPTER 20
CALLIOPE

When I wake up, I'm wrapped around Michael like a Snuggie. As I untangle from him, he opens his eyes.

"Good morning," he murmurs.

Not sure why I blush, but I do, and I also cover my boobs with the blanket, as though we didn't—

"You want to go to the bathroom first?" he asks. "Or should I?"

How is he awake enough to ponder such difficult choices?

"You go." This way I can put on some clothes in the meanwhile.

He leaps out of the bed like he's already had two espressos, and I enjoy watching his naked butt and thighs flexing with every step.

Once I have a minute of privacy, I dress and ponder the implications of last night—a.k.a. the best sex I've ever had, or BS for short.

Right before BS went down, Michael implied that

despite having a rule against dating, he'd make an exception for me. Of course, it wasn't crystal clear if that was his asking me to go steady, or stating that it's a remote possibility.

Either way, what I also don't know is whether I want us to date. As soon as he meets my family, he'll realize that—

"The bathroom is yours," Michael says, startling me.

When I slant a gaze his way, he—unfortunately—has a robe on.

"Can you order room service?" I ask.

He nods, and I hurry into the bathroom to perform my morning routine.

When I come out, he's dressed and just finishing a call.

"I was able to move up our flight," he says, pocketing his phone.

I cock my head questioningly.

"I'll feel better about dealing with the stalker on my home turf," he explains.

Oh, shit. He fucked me so thoroughly that I completely forgot about the danger we're in. Now that I remember, I'm not sure if I'd feel safer back home and I tell him so, reminding him that my dressing room was invaded, and maybe my apartment.

"That's why I want you to stay with me," he says. "I live in a private community and am surrounded by nosy neighbors. There's no way the stalker can—"

"Hold on." I stare at him. "Are you asking me to move in with you?"

There's a knock on the door. "Room service."

Michael lets the woman in, and I see that he not only ordered food for the two of us, but also for my rats—which is the most persuasive argument he could've made for this crazy "move in together" idea.

"Yes," Michael says when we're alone again. "I do want you to move in."

I squeeze my breakfast quesadilla so hard a glob of Monterey Jack Cheese drips onto my plate. Wolfgang swoops in and wolfs it down.

Meine Liebe, tell him you'll move in if he can guarantee that every day will start with this much premium cheese.

I clear my throat. "Don't you think us shacking up is moving our relationship—or whatever this is—a bit too fast?"

He frowns. "Who says 'shacking up' these days?"

"Moving in is a serious step," I say, ignoring the jab.

"I'm not asking you to move in because we're dating." He picks up his spoon and stabs it into his unappetizing-looking bowl of plain oats. "It's to keep you safe."

Huh. Did I misunderstand? My pits begin to sweat. "So… we're not dating?"

His eyes gleam. "Of course we are. Didn't we establish that last night?"

Whew. That would've been embarrassing to get wrong. And more than a little disappointing. "You said 'exceptions can be made,'" I remind him. "That's not exactly—"

"Calliope," he says somberly. "I have a big announcement I'd like to make. Pay attention, please."

I blow out my breath. "Okay, okay, I get it—"

"Will you do me the honor of dating me?" he says in that same tone. "For real this time?"

Fuck. Now that the question is out, I feel a full-fledged panic, which is very stupid, considering how badly I wanted it a second ago.

"I'll date you under one condition," I blurt. "You meet my family next Friday."

The logic—if there's any to this madness—is that if he can't handle the lunacy that is my family, it's better to know now. It's early enough that my heart won't be in danger. Too much danger, at least.

Yes. I can't believe I didn't think of this idea sooner.

Michael stares at me. "Isn't 'meeting the parents' also a step that happens much further on in relationships?"

"Sometimes," I say. "In our case, my family thinks we've been dating all this time. Except for my sister Seraphina, who knows the truth—but she kept saying we'd end up together anyway. Meeting them all will clear the air." Or put a nail in the coffin of this relationship.

"Okay. I'll meet the Klaunbuts." He pronounces my last name in the German fashion I invented.

I sigh. "It's fine. You can say 'clown butts.' Even to their faces. That's what they go by."

He nods, then looks out the window, eyes widening.

At first, my heart sinks as I picture the stalker spelunking into our room.

But this isn't that.

It's a bird sitting on a windowsill.

A gorgeous specimen with a blue-gray back, white underpants, and a black head.

"That's a peregrine falcon," Michael says reverently.

Ah, right. He's a bird watcher. But… "What's it doing here in Manhattan?"

Until now, I thought big cities only had two types of birds—pigeons and sparrows—but this is neither of those.

Michael fishes out his phone and takes a picture. "I've heard of people spotting them here. We're very lucky."

A few of my rats produce short squeaks of disapproval, while others escalate them to long squeaks, which is their version of "go to the dick."

"I don't think my rats think us so lucky," I say.

Michael waves that away. "Rats aren't the peregrine's primary food source."

I scoff. "That just means they'll eat one when there's nothing tastier around."

I gather my little ones into their carrier. We're leaving soon anyway, and this way, they'll feel safer.

Michael takes another photo. "Being the fastest animal on the planet, the peregrine falcon is famous for its hunting skills. They can even catch other birds."

"Wow." Can he spout facts about any random bird?

"They can also fly fifteen-and-a-half thousand miles a year to migrate between continents," he continues. "They nest on high cliffs or buildings, and they mate for life."

Ah. That last bit makes me almost sympathetic to this rat-killing machine.

With a whoosh of powerful wings, the peregrine falcon takes flight—and I silently hope he's spotted a pigeon as opposed to something cute and cuddly, like a rat.

"Did that make your trip?" I ask. "Or was it that big check last night?"

Michael's eyes darken as he turns toward me. "Something last night made my year… but it wasn't the check."

Great. Now I'm blushing. Again.

———

"How big of a truck do we need to rent in order to move your stuff to my place?" Michael asks me once we land in Florida.

I chuckle. "I shared a room with my sister until recently. My things can fit in the trunk of a car." And an embarrassing amount of my worldly possessions are actually with me right now.

"Great." He helps me carry said possessions over to his car, and then we head to my place, where we park next to the lake, the view of which I will probably miss.

"Do you only like birds?" I ask Michael and then gesture at the giant gator who is warming himself nearby. "Or would a close relative of theirs also interest you?"

He shakes his head. "No wings, no interest."

"What about the ostrich? They have no wings."

He scratches his head. "They have vestigial wings.

Though it's a moot point because I like seeing birds in their natural habitat, and we're not in Africa."

With an eyeroll, I lead him to my place and show him the floorboards that I thought were messed with.

"This used to be Ted's place, right?" Michael asks, crouching down to examine the floor.

I nod.

"Could it be he left something here, like drugs, and then snuck in to get them back?"

I shrug. "I don't know the guy, but it sounds possible."

Michael removes a couple of floorboards and exhales in disappointment. "Nothing there now."

I give him another shrug and go to pack up my stuff —which takes all of twenty minutes.

———

"Wow, your community is very nice," I say when we drive through the fancy gate.

There are herons and giant ducks swimming in a nearby lake, as well as what Michael tells me are snake-birds, along with a whole bunch of other fowl.

"Living here has been very helpful ever since the viral video business started," he says after he identifies each bird for me. "Security will not allow any media vultures to get inside—or to even loiter near the gate."

Huh. "You would scare them away anyway."

He shrugs. "I'm glad to be spared the headache."

We park on the driveway of a house that is so large it is just a couple of bricks short of being a mansion. I gape at the grandeur as Michael gets the door for me. When we step inside, he says, "Welcome to my humble abode."

"Right. Humble." The ceilings are about twenty feet tall, there are gorgeous paintings and statues of birds all over the walls, and the furniture looks like it jumped straight out of a European furniture catalog.

"Your rats can have the parlor room," he says, leading me over to a space bigger than the apartment I just vacated.

I let the rats out and everyone seems happy, except for Lenin, who looks at me reproachfully.

Tovarisch, you're turning me, the proletari-rat, into a fat bourgeoisie.

"Where am *I* going to stay?" I ask Michael.

Please say "my bed."

"I have two guest rooms," he says. "Let's see which you prefer."

I'm both impressed and disappointed. Also, I was wrong before. This *is* a mansion. "Seems like us mascots don't get paid as much as the players," I muse as we walk from room to luxurious room.

Michael grunts. "Given how much I hated the idea of Florida, they had to give me a very competitive salary to lure me here."

I spin around to glare at him. "What could you possibly hate about living in Florida?"

"Fucking sunlight." He folds his pinky finger. "It blinds you, gives you cancer, and wakes you too early in the morning." He folds his ring finger. "Fucking grass. It's everywhere, and has snakes lurking in it, and pesticides, and bugs that are resistant to said pesticides." He folds his middle finger. "Fucking ocean. It's wet and too salty, and people drown in it all the time, and fish pee in it. And there are sharks that—"

"Jeesh, stop." I bet he was going to use up all his ten fingers, and maybe go on to toes. "There must be things you've grown to like."

His eyes gleam. "You mean... besides certain special people?"

I nod, my chest bubbly all of a sudden.

He purses his lips in such a way that makes me want to kiss them. "The birds, obviously." He walks me over to a big window facing a forest and looks into a telescope for a few seconds. An almost-boyish grin appears on his face and makes something ache in the pit of my belly as he says, "Ethan and Mo are feeding Eye right this moment." He pulls me over. "Have a look."

I do, and it's cute, or as cute as watching a bird puke food into a smaller bird's beak can possibly be.

"Do hawks mate for life?" I pull away from the telescope.

"This type does," he says. "Which is all the more impressive given the fact that they are solitary birds."

Huh. "Is it true they can mate mid-air?" Because that sounds pretty cool, especially if—

"No," he says. "When the male wants to woo a female, he'll dive bomb to show her how good a hunter he is, and then tackle her. What follows merely looks like they're doing it in the air. But, in reality, if she's down to fuck, they'll do it on a perch, on the ground, or in their nest."

Why does the idea of getting tackled sound kind of hot? Do I have a bird brain?

My phone rings, sparing me from dwelling on more questions in the same vein.

"It's my sister," I tell Michael as I pick up.

Nodding knowingly, he walks out of earshot.

"Hey," I say.

"Don't you 'hey' me," Seraphina says sternly. "Once again, our family has to learn about you from viral videos."

"What?"

"The way your boyfriend almost killed the Yeti mascot," she says. "And that kiss. I couldn't *bear* any of it."

I don't ask her which of the many kisses she's talking about because that would just be making her point for her.

"I will make it up to you and everyone else in the family," I say.

"You will?" She sounds pretty skeptical.

"Are Mom and Dad having the usual Friday night dinner?"

"No way," she squeaks. "You can't mean it. You're really going to—"

"I am. Assuming it's okay with Mom."

There's a sound of running on the other end of the call, and I hear Seraphina asking Mom if she wants to meet my Boo Boo.

Something clanks loudly. Seraphina shouts something like "that's my phone."

"Calliope," Mom says, the excitement in her voice a little disturbing. "If you don't bring your boyfriend over after teasing me like this, I will not speak to you for a month."

"Hold on." I locate Michael and mute my phone to ask if he'd like to go to dinner with my family on Friday.

He smiles. "I'd love to meet your family."

Yeah, sure. There go the famous last words in our budding relationship.

CHAPTER 21
CALLIOPE

I t doesn't take me long to arrange my stuff in the guest room of my choice, though I feel depressed at the thought of actually sleeping here instead of next to Michael... assuming that is the arrangement he has in mind.

Spotting what's left of my bear suit, I give Coach a call, and he reassures me that Michael already told him about the loss, and that a new suit will be waiting in my dressing room.

When I'm done with everything, Michael offers to cook us dinner.

"Can I help?" I ask.

"If you wish." He leads me to the kitchen, where he has me watch as he expertly chops up mushrooms and then fries them without any hint of needing my help.

"I didn't realize you needed me for moral support," I grumble as my stomach rumbles from the earthy, delicious scent.

Michael chuckles. "Do you know how to make *vareniki*?"

"I don't know what that is."

"A Ukrainian staple," he says. "Similar to *pelmeni*, but with more options when it comes to fillings."

"Oh, that explains it," I say with a hint of an eyeroll. "What's *pelmeni* then?" Another nickname he plans to bestow upon me?

"They're a type of Russian dumpling." He pulls out a packet of flour from a drawer that is so high up I'd need a step stool to reach it. "They originated in Siberia and were likely inspired by Chinese wontons."

"Oh. That sounds delicious."

And hey, "dumpling" can be a term of endearment, though I strongly prefer "little bird."

"Both dishes are delicious. *Pelmeni* are always filled with meat, but *vareniki* can have all sorts of fillings— and my favorite is mushrooms." He starts kneading the dough with his strong hands, which, for some odd reason, makes my boobs extremely jealous.

Watching all this from my shoulder, Wolfgang chirps.

"He wants to know if the various fillings for *vareniki* include cheese," I say with a grin.

"Actually, yes," Michael says. "One of the sweet varieties is filled with farmers' cheese and sugar. I'm not sure if a rat would like them."

I glance at Wolfgang, whose eyes are wide.

Meine Liebe, so long as it's filled with some type of cheese, I'd eat anything, even a bullet.

"This is my favorite part." Michael grabs a rolling

pin, sprinkles flour over the table, and starts rolling the dough, his naked, hairy, muscular forearms driving me insane in the process.

"Here." He hands me a glass and takes one for himself. "Stamp circles with me." He shows me how, and I help while my heart hammers in my chest for no obvious reason.

"Now take the mushrooms and stick them in the center of each circle," he says, demonstrating.

A part of me realizes that his words and actions are not sensual, but the rest of me reacts as though the word "mushroom" were a euphemism for his cock and "center" for my pussy.

"Yes," he says approvingly when I penetrate the dough with the fungi. "Just like that."

Shit. I never knew cooking could make you so ravenous... for a dick. But here we are.

"Now we make half-moons," Michael says, cutting through my horny haze. He folds one of the circles we made, then pushes the edges together with his fingers. And is it just me, or do said edges look suspiciously like pussy lips?

Anyway, I somehow glue together a dozen dumplings without climbing Michael like a tree.

He then boils water, tosses in the dumplings, and waits until they float to the top, which means they are done.

"Now we eat them with sour cream." He fills two plates and hands one to me, along with a fork.

When I bite a piece of the dumpling, the savory

flavor explodes in my mouth, making me moan in pleasure.

"Wow," I say after I swallow. "That was the best thing I've had in my mouth in a long time."

Michael arches an eyebrow, and I blush as I realize how dirty my words sounded.

"So, you're not a fan of Florida," I say, desperate to change the subject. "What else do you dislike?"

He cocks his head. "How much time do we have?"

"The list is *that* long?"

He scratches his head. "I don't like it when people are being stupid. I'm not a fan of when someone shows me pictures from their vacation. I hate it when—"

As promised, the list continues for a while, and it makes me feel more and more anxious about the prospect of Michael meeting my family. I mean, "being stupid" is open to interpretation, but I'm sure someone —probably my older brother—will fit whatever definition Michael has. Someone might also—

"Oh, and the last one," Michael says. "I want to murder anyone who clips their nails on the subway."

"Are you sure that's all?" I ask sarcastically.

"Well, I guess toenails too," he says with a straight face.

I roll my eyes. "Did that really happen?"

He nods. "Brooklyn. The R-line. A woman clipped her toenails and then stunk up the subway car with nail polish."

Wow. "Okay, we may be in agreement on that one. I wouldn't like it either." And I guess it's the silver lining to the fact that we don't have subways here in Florida.

"It was disgusting." Now that his plate is clean, Michael puts down his fork. "And I'm sorry I brought it up at the table."

"Oh, my appetite is unaffected." For food and for a certain someone, despite how long his "dislikes" list is.

Before he can read the latter on my face, I stuff my mouth with my last dumpling and do my best not to moan as I chew it.

I must be chomping in a weird way or something because Michael watches my mouth very intently, like he's trying to read my lips for some hidden message.

"What would you like to do after dinner?" he finally asks.

I shrug. "Watch some Netflix?" And then, fingers crossed, chill?

"Good idea." He takes his phone out and looks something up. "How about the older *Suicide Squad*? We liked the newer one, so…"

"Sure. How bad can it be?"

As it turns out, the answer is "very." And yet I can't bring myself to care because I'm sitting on the couch next to Michael, and the heat of his body melts something in my nether regions, turning me on so much that even a weirdly silver-toothed Joker isn't spoiling it.

As the action on the screen picks up, Michael wraps his arm around me—which instantly adds at least two stars to my hypothetical review of the film. A little deeper in, Michael pulls me toward him, making me realize two things: we're officially snuggling, and relatedly, this movie deserves on Oscar.

I float on a happy cloud until the credits start to roll,

at which point I face Michael and catch him examining my lips… again.

I moisten said lips. "Did you like it?"

His reply is to crush his mouth against mine.

Oh, my. The kiss is hungry, passionate, and not at all what I'd expect from someone who offered me the guestroom to sleep in.

A tiny moan of pleasure escapes my lips and is promptly swallowed by his.

In an eyeblink, we're kissing while standing and tugging on each other's clothes. In two eyeblinks, a trail of those clothes leads all the way to Michael's bedroom, where he lays me on the sheets and devours my pussy like a man possessed.

"I want to make you come a hundred more times," he growls once I'm buzzing from a post-orgasm glow. "Maybe a thousand."

I manage to open my eyes. "That's pretty ambitious, even for you."

He shuts me up with a kiss and proceeds to work on his lofty goal until I lose count of the number of times I come.

———

The next morning, I wake up to the sound of nearby grunts.

Huh. Why am I hearing sexy noises that do not involve me? Is Michael jerking off after yesterday's sex marathon?

No.

Impossible.

I sit up and see that he's not spanking any monkeys. Instead, he's doing push-ups by the bed, which is an even weirder thing to do first thing in the morning.

And did I mention that he's naked? With muscles glistening and with beads of sweat rolling down his taut skin.

And that butt.

Don't get me started on that butt.

Suddenly, what seemed like a crazy idea just a moment ago—masturbating first thing in the morning—sounds like a very reasonable and practical way to start the day.

Without intending to, I exhale a tormented breath.

Michael stops the exercise and leaps to his feet. "Morning," he says, breathing as evenly as if he'd been on a gentle stroll. "Did I wake you?"

"No." Unless a sexual awakening counts. "What are you doing?"

He walks over to the doorframe and grabs onto a bar attached there, one I didn't notice before.

"A workout." He pulls his massive body up with his naked back to me, and every single muscle on it throbs with tension… or maybe it's my pussy projecting a bit. "Exercising while fasting enhances fat utilization and builds endurance."

"Fat?" He's got zero of that on his shredded body. "Endurance?" Is that how he is able to fuck me so much?

"It also wakes me up much faster," he says as he pulls himself up for the twentieth time.

"I'll grant you that one." His working out has sure woken *me* up pretty fast.

He lets go of the bar, turns my way, and shocks me with the sight of his cock half-mast—presumably from exercise. "Do you want to give this a try?"

The cock? No. He's gesturing at the bar.

"You're kidding, right?" I never realized keeping eye contact is this difficult when a man's cock is out.

"Don't worry," Michael says. "I'll spot you."

I shake my head. "I need to brush my teeth first."

"Ah, sure. I also do that before working out. I find the minty flavor of toothpaste just arousing enough to get me ready for exercise."

And I find his exercising arousing, which I think is the circle of life.

Grabbing my bra and panties, I sprint to the bathroom, put them on, and then do my business.

When I come out, Michael is on the floor again, doing something for his washboard abs. His legs are in the air, cock and balls still out, and he's twisting from side to side while holding a dumbbell.

"What is that called?" I ask breathlessly. And hey, a question is better than kneeling and putting that cock in my mouth, or licking those balls, all of which is what I really want to do.

"Russian twists," he says, again not the least bit out of breath.

I grin. "I think you can just call them twists."

He leaps to his feet, cock swinging. "Which do you want to start with, a pushup or a pullup?"

Are those the only two options? "I don't think I can do either."

"Yes, you can." He explains to me how to do an assisted pushup—with knees on the floor—and I surprise myself when I'm able to do a few.

"See?" he says. "You're stronger than you thought."

I shrug, my breath decidedly uneven. "That still doesn't mean I can do a pullup."

"You can, if I assist you."

I look at the bar skeptically. "How is that going to work?"

When he explains, I suddenly want to do a pullup, and badly.

Apparently, to help someone do pullups, you hold their legs in a very sensual-sounding manner, and when Michael does it to me, I channel the surge of lust into my arms and back muscles, which lets me do the impossible: pull myself up five times.

"See?" he says when I'm panting afterward. "I knew you could do it."

"Yeah." I bite my lip. "I think I deserve a reward."

His eyes grow hooded, and his cock instantly hardens. "What did you have in mind?"

"I want you to fuck me while fasting," I say huskily. "I hear it has all sorts of benefits."

He's upon me in one leap, and then we're on the bed, with Michael finally out of breath as he pounds into me, over and over again.

"Wow," I say when I finally catch *my* breath in the aftermath. "That last one was so good I thought I'd faint."

"You might be feeling faint from hunger," he says with a frown. "Stay here. I'll bring you some breakfast."

Breakfast in bed? "Sure." Especially since I don't think I can move.

He comes back with a tray that has two cups of tea, two bowls of buckwheat porridge, and enough berries to run a smoothie bar for a year.

"Thanks." I dip my spoon into the bowl and taste the breakfast. "Huh. This goes well with a workout." In that it tastes healthy and not like something I'd want to eat on a regular basis.

Michael gets in bed next to me, improving the meal considerably.

I didn't think we'd both be having breakfast in bed today. It's not something I've ever done with a man before, but I love it, and not just because lounging about is the opposite of pushups. In fact, I feel so amazing a twinge of dread intrudes into my thoughts when I recall that we're planning to meet my family this Friday—which might just be the end of whatever is happening between us.

Which would be a fucking shame.

"This is nice," Michael says, adding "psychic" to his plethora of gifts.

"Why did that sound like you wanted to say 'nice, but...'?" I sip the tea, finding it delicious.

"*But* we have to go to work."

Oh. "Right. You have practice." And I do too, even if mine involves practicing throwing pies at people's faces.

With great reluctance, we leave the bed, get dressed,

feed my rats, allow Wolfgang to perch on my shoulder, and make the short drive.

As we walk together from the parking lot, Michael grabs my hand—which causes a frenzy with the media people that are waiting for us by the arena entrance. A frenzy that matches the backflips a bunch of horny butterflies are doing in my stomach.

"See you on the ice," he murmurs and gives me a kiss when we reach the locker room.

"Get a room," says Dante, who happens to be passing by.

"How about a coffin?" Michael growls back.

Dante blinks. "Why would you get yourselves a coffin?"

Michael glares at him. "It's your vampire ass that will need a coffin to sleep in if you don't shut the fuck up."

Muttering something about it still not making any sense, Dante strides into the locker room while Michael gives me another kiss before following his maybe-friend.

When I get to my dressing room, I see the new suit, so I put it on and glance into the mirror to get into character. "Roar. Mr. Bloom is horny, and hungry. He wants manuka honey all over the big jugs of his Pookie-poo so he can lick it off with his giant, hairy cock."

Wolfgang narrows his eyes at me in the mirror, like he thinks that wasn't my best effort.

"This is harder to do now that I don't refer to myself as Bearman," I explain. "It just wouldn't feel right, knowing that Michael wouldn't like it."

Meine Liebe, you can do whatever you want and then smooth things over with a shot of fondue cheese.

––––––

After the training is over, Michael takes me and Wolfgang out to lunch, where he has to tip the waiters extra to turn a blind eye to the rat at our table. Once we're back at Michael's house, we both get on our laptops—with Michael working on something for his foundation and me searching for an opportunity to perform with my rats.

"Do you want to order in, or should I make something?" Michael asks around the time when my eyes get tired from staring at the screen.

"Whatever you prefer," I tell him. I mean, I loved his cooking, but I don't want to impose… any more than I already have.

"I'll make my own version of *solyanka*," he says. "Which is a type of soup that is hearty enough to be a complete meal."

"Sounds great. Meanwhile, I'll go spend some quality time with my rats."

I walk over to their room. The rats are excited to see both me and Wolfgang, at least if I go by how they eagerly zoom all over the place and how happily they hop around.

I give everyone snacks. Lenin asks for seconds and then thirds.

Tovarisch, the corruption of the rat proletariat is now complete. Next thing you know, I'll be craving McNuggets, investing in the capitalist stock market, and watching The Kardashians.

"Hey," Michael says, walking into the room. "Dinner is ready."

I follow him to the kitchen, where I taste his *solyanka* —which vaguely reminds me of a stew but with pickles and olives, a flavor profile that combines with the other ingredients to create a surprisingly delicious result.

"What movie should we watch today?" Michael asks as we finish eating.

I shrug. "How about you choose?"

I honestly don't care, so long as we do afterward what we did last night.

"How about *Chip 'n Dale: Rescue Rangers*?" he asks.

"Why?" It's oddly unsexy. Is he trying to avoid what happened last night?

"I thought you'd like it," he says. "It's got rats."

"No, it doesn't. They're chipmunks. A different species altogether." And not nearly as cute.

"Okay, we can watch something else. Maybe something with Russian spies?"

"No, *Chip 'n Dale* is fine." A movie with Russian spies will no doubt have a hot female lead à la Scarlett Johansson, and that will make me too jealous to enjoy myself.

We cozy up with each other on the couch, and it makes me so horny you'd think the movie featured Chippendales, the strip club, instead of detective rodents.

When the credits roll, Michael clears his throat. "That was surprisingly good. Right?"

Nodding, I turn to him. "I *really* enjoyed myself."

"You think you did." His black eyes gleam. "But in reality, your enjoyment is only about to begin." With that, he picks me up, carries me into his bedroom, and fucks me so properly and thoroughly that I might as well admit it.

I'm completely and utterly ruined for other men.

———

The days that follow are blissfully similar. I wake up to a naked Michael exercising, join him, have a dozen orgasms, go to work, enjoy a home-cooked meal and a movie, and then more orgasms follow. The only negative is that as time passes, I dread his meeting my family more and more. I also illogically dread the resolution of my stalker situation, as that could bring about the end of this blissful coexistence.

"You know, we don't have to meet my family tonight," I tell Michael as we drive home from work on Friday. "I'm craving *vareniki*, and my mom doesn't know how to make them."

He frowns. "Didn't you tell your parents to expect us?"

"Sure, but—"

"No buts," he says sternly. "You told them I'd be there, and I won't offend them by flaking."

"Oh, they'll be sure that it's my fault," I say.

He pulls up to a flower shop. "I can't take any chances."

With a sigh, I ask him why we're getting flowers.

"For your parents, of course," he says. "I'm also going to get a box of candy."

"Oh?"

My guess is the candy is symbolic. To slightly paraphrase Forrest Gump, life around Michael is like a box of chocolates.

You never know how many orgasms you're going to get.

CHAPTER 22
MICHAEL

"There." Calliope gestures at the circus parking lot.

So, she was serious. Her family really does live at the circus.

Once we're parked, I get the box of candy and bouquet of flowers from the trunk while Calliope sighs again.

"I told you, you didn't need to bring anything," she says for the umpteenth time.

"And I told you—Russians can't go to dinner empty-handed." And no one really should.

She leads me through the stage area, and among all the oddities, the one that catches my attention is an old woman walking on tightrope near the ceiling.

"That's my grandmother," Calliope explains.

I look for a net under the rope and find none. "Does she have some sort of a safety harness attaching her to the ceiling?"

Because I can't see one of those either.

Calliope sighs heavily. "She claims she doesn't need such silliness now that she's eighty years old."

I point at the people practicing right below, on whom the grandmother would land if she were to take a misstep: a guy swallowing a sword, a fire breather, and a mime. "What about them? They all seem too young to be killed by her fall—or to be traumatized by—"

"You're preaching to the choir," Calliope says. "And if you find a way to convince my grandmother to take safety precautions, the rest of the family will give you a medal."

"Hey, cousin!" shouts the mime with a big grin. "Is that your new boyfriend?"

Calliope tsks-tsks. "You're in full costume. Are you allowed to talk?"

The mime jerks off her right glove. "There. Please don't tell anyone I broke character."

Calliope snorts. "I do have WMO on speed dial, so…"

The mime pales. "Seriously. I didn't—"

"If you can get everyone here to the dinner table, I'll never tell a soul," Calliope says.

"So," I say when we're out of earshot of the neurotic mime. "You're not just mean to me."

Calliope glances at me. "Was I mean? The last thing I want is for her to give me the silent treatment again."

I narrow my eyes. "Was that a mime joke?"

She nods.

"And what's WMO?" I can't help but ask. "Another joke? It sounds like some sort of mime mafia."

"World Mime Organization," she replies. "But hey, mime mafia sounds like an unspeakable horror."

I snort.

"They use guns with silencers," she says and continues making mime-related jokes as we walk up to a hallway with a bunch of doors.

"That one." Calliope gestures at number ten. "That's where I lived until recently."

She knocks.

No one answers, though I can hear boisterous laughter and loud conversations happening inside.

"Typical." Calliope pulls out a key and opens the door.

The sounds grow louder, and we enter, ending up in a kitchen. The first person I notice is an older woman who looks so much like Calliope that it is easy to guess this is her mother. She's sitting in a split, a chopping knife in her hand and a cutting board on the floor next to her. A man standing near her is juggling vegetables. Calliope's father?

"Aromatics," the woman says.

The juggler adroitly tosses an onion in the air in such a way that it lands squarely on the cutting board. Then he does the same with a clove of garlic.

"Thanks, honey," the woman says and starts chopping without coming out of the split.

"Hi, Mom. Hi, Dad," Calliope says.

Clearly startled, her dad drops a turnip, and her mom leaps to her feet, both examining me with unabashed curiosity.

"Hi," I say, and thrust the flowers at her mom.

"This is for you." I give her dad the chocolates and curse myself for not bringing a bottle of vodka as well.

"You must be Boo Boo," Calliope's dad says.

"No. Just Boo. Singular," Calliope corrects. "Right, Boo?"

I grunt in the affirmative.

"Just Boo?" Her mom frowns. "But the internet—"

"Would have you believe I'm Honey," Calliope says. "When in reality, I'm his Pit-Check-Uh."

"It's pronounced *ptichka*." I smile at the parents. "It means little bird."

"Aww," the mom says. "That's much better than 'Honey.'"

"But just one Boo is a downgrade from Boo Boo," the dad chimes in. "Though I'm sure you'll come up with a better endearment for him over time."

"I prefer it when she calls me Michael," I say.

"Well, it's nice to meet you, Michael," the dad says. "I'm Zephyr."

Should I tell him that's a name of a Russian confectionary that's very similar to meringue?

"And I'm Xanthe," the mom says.

"It's a pleasure," I reply. On a whim, I take her hand and give it a light kiss.

Xanthe gasps, grabs her daughter by her shoulder, and very loudly whispers, "You'd better marry this one. We could use a Klaunbut with manners."

"He wouldn't be a Klaunbut," Zephyr says. "She'd be a—

"Mom, Dad, please stop," Calliope says, her cheeks

burning. "This is our first official date, so talking about marriage is—"

"Hello," says a guy who seems to have materialized out of thin air. "I'm Calliope's brother. I'm sure she's mentioned me."

Actually, she hasn't talked about her family all that much, but I'm not about to tell them that. "I'm Michael." I extend my hand.

"Tortellini," the brother says, and everyone around him groans.

Like the round Italian *pelmeni*-like things?

"He's actually called Torey," Calliope says with an eyeroll.

"But Tortellini is my stage name." Torey / Tortellini shakes my hand, and as he pulls it away, a face-down playing card remains on my palm somehow.

"Quick," Tortellini says. "What card do you think that is?"

I peer at it. "The Ace of Spades?"

Looking triumphant, Tortellini tells me to turn the card over.

Well, I'll be damned. It *is* the Ace of Spades. "So... you're the magician of the family?"

He frowns. "My name didn't give it away?"

"No." But it does make me hungrier for dinner.

"Haven't you ever heard of Houdini?" he demands. "Or Slydini? Or Cardini? Or Cantini?"

"Only the first one," I say. "Whenever someone escapes a tight situation on the ice, Coach tells them they've 'pulled a Houdini.'"

Tortellini nods with great enthusiasm. "He should

use the others too. If someone is very sneaky with the puck, he could say they've pulled a Slydini, and if—"

"How about you let me introduce Michael to more of the family," Calliope says sternly to her brother and drags me away before there's an answer.

"Sorry about Torey," she whispers. "Magic to him is what rats are to me."

I wave it away. "I respect passion, and there seems to be a lot of it in your family."

"Sure. Let's call it passion," she says, stopping next to a door on which she knocks.

"Come in!" shouts a female voice.

"Are you decent?" Calliope shouts back.

"Sure. Why not?"

Calliope opens the door. "This used to be my room." She points at the ceiling. "And that's my sister and former roommate."

I shouldn't be surprised by anything at this point, but it's still a shock to find said sister hanging upside down, like a bat.

"I'm Seraphina." She extends me her hand, and I shake it, a surprisingly disorienting gesture when the other person is in that position.

"I'm Michael."

"I know." Seraphina waggles her eyebrows. "Calliope has told me all about the *koala-ty* time you've had together."

I blink. "Koala-ty?"

Calliope groans. "Seraphina doesn't know how much you hate bear-related jokes, so that was an attempt at one, I think."

"I've used up all the best ones already," Seraphina says with a pout. "Now I'm scraping the bottom of the *bear-rel*."

"And that's our cue to leave," Calliope says sternly and drags me out of the room.

"Sorry about her," she says. "She didn't know about your thing."

I shrug. "When the puns are *that* bad, I don't feel offended. I actually pity the punster." Especially if he's a guy, because I'd still punch him, on principle.

"All right," Calliope says. "Let me introduce you to a few more people."

"A few" turns out to be an understatement. I meet so many Klaunbuts I barely remember their names, and even their circus specialties start to blur.

"Dinner is ready!" calls Xanthe.

Calliope leads me to the circus cafeteria, where someone has pulled all the tables together into one giant, circular arrangement.

"Sit next to us," Calliope's parents say to her. "We want to get to know Michael, and we haven't seen you in forever."

So we sit near them, and they pepper me with questions about hockey and growing up in Russia until I steer the conversation back to their family and, by extension, the circus.

Turns out, it's been a family business for generations. At one point in time, they were carnies, with all that it implied. For instance, a great-grandmother of Calliope's was a bearded woman who was married to both halves of conjoined twins. Said husbands shared a torso and therefore a penis, but had separate heads and personalities.

My head spins just picturing that.

Eventually, the focus shifts from me to their regular family banter and bickering, giving me a chance to simply eat and observe the Klaunbut clan. As I do, I can't help but feel an ache in my chest, alongside something uncomfortably like self-pity tinged with envy. I'm not sure if these people realize just how lucky they are. As an orphan who is pretty much alone in this world, this here is my idea of heaven, and I'd give anything to—

Calliope grips my forearm. "I'm so sorry I dragged you here. I can tell you're having a horrible time."

Fuck. She's misinterpreted my expression. "That's not true," I tell her. "All is well."

She tightens her grip. "It's Voldemort, isn't it?"

"Who?"

She gestures at a woman with a snake around her neck. "That's my aunt, Azalea, but some of us call her Voldemort on account of the snake she always walks around with. The snake's name is Nancy, by the way, but should have been Nagini."

I snort. "Should a person with a rat on her shoulder really throw stones?"

"Well, if you're not bothered by Voldemort, then what's wrong? Is it my youngest sister?" She gestures at a young woman who looks a lot like her—except for the fact that she's eating while twisted into a pretzel-like shape that doesn't look beneficial for digestion. "I keep telling her that contortionist shit is horror-movie creepy."

I have no idea how I can explain the yearnings her big family makes me feel, so when my phone dings with an email, I'm grateful for a moment of reprieve. When I see what the email is about, though, my whole body goes on full alert.

The sender is the manager from the hotel—and she's finally come through with the security video footage that I've been waiting for. The footage that will tell me who Calliope's stalker is.

Now, I know I probably shouldn't play this video here at the dinner table, but I can't help myself. My finger clicks on it, and I watch intently, at first unable to process what I'm seeing.

Once I do, my hands ball into tight fists and a rage unlike any I've ever felt rushes through my blood.

I never for a second thought the stalker would be someone I knew. But it is—and the fucking bastard doesn't know it yet, but he's a dead man.

CHAPTER 23
CALLIOPE

The sweet potato in my mouth turns into packing peanuts as I watch Michael's expression turn thunderous. And then he leaps to his feet. "I have to go."

What the hell? I mean, I know he's not having a good time—those weird facial expressions made that clear—but why is he so angry?

Because that's what he seems to be. Angry. So much so, that as he stomps out of the cafeteria, his hands are balled into fists and his jaw ticks. If he punches a random Klaunbut on his way out, I won't be surprised in the least.

"Is everything okay?" Mom asks with a worried expression when Michael is gone.

"Does it look like things are okay?" I retort.

Mom shrugs. "I don't know him as well as you do."

My chest aches, and a pressure is building behind my eyes. "I'm not sure I know him all that well myself."

Deep down, a part of me had been convinced that he'd like my family, and we'd live happily ever after.

How stupid.

I'm obviously cursed to lose boyfriends as soon as I introduce them to this literal circus. And I was also stupid to think that this would hurt less because I had him meet everyone at the very beginning of our relationship. I imagined it would be like ripping off a Band-Aid in the worst case, but this feels more like ripping off a finger.

Seraphina plops into the chair Michael vacated. "What happened?"

"I don't know." Not exactly. The trigger for him leaving could have been so many weird behaviors around us that it's a wonder he lasted as long as he did.

"You think this is like your asshole of an ex situation?" she whispers.

"What else?" Even people as grouchy as Michael don't just leave in the middle of dinner for no reason, and in this case, the reason is obvious.

"Well, fuck him," Seraphina says.

Yeah. I did. Seemingly countless times.

"Better you be rid of him now," she continues. "Before you get too attached."

Yeah, except it's too late for that one.

I put my fork down. "Sorry, everyone. I think I'd better go."

"Yeah," Dad says. "Smart. Go after your Boo."

Mine. Sure.

Pushing to my feet, I make my exit, and though I

didn't just have a one-night stand or anything close to it, the term "walk of shame" is perfect for my current situation. Everyone saw Michael storm out, and now they're looking at me with expressions that range from judgy to pitying.

Once I'm outside, the pressure behind my eyes grows stronger, especially when I realize that I don't have a ride back.

My nose makes a sniffle.

No.

I'm not going to cry.

Screw that.

Getting my phone out, I summon an Uber. I'm about to stuff it back into my purse when it rings.

My heart leaps inside my chest. Could it be Michael calling to apologize? Then again, he's more likely to ask me to move my shit out of his house.

It's not Michael, though. The number is a 212 area code, which I believe is New York.

"Hello?" I clear my throat to make sure what I say next doesn't sound as miserable as that first greeting. "Calliope speaking."

"Good evening, Calliope. This is Maximilian Bowman," says a booming voice.

Maximilian Bowman? I strain my brain until I recall that he's the husband of Sugar, the woman who was the first to ask for my business card at Michael's fundraiser, and who got a napkin with some scribbles instead.

"Hi," I say. "We met at the fundraiser, right?"

"Correct," Maximilian—or is it Mr. Bowman?—says.

"I've been thinking about that outstanding rat show of yours, and when a spot opened at my theater, I—"

"You own a theater?" I blurt, and then want to smack myself for interrupting the man.

"Apologies," he says. "I figured my name spoke for itself. I don't own The Jewel outright, but I am the largest stakeholder and—"

The Jewel? That's one of the biggest—

"Is this a good time to talk?" he asks. "Perhaps over video?"

Shit. I need to focus. "Yes, Mr. Bowman. So long as you don't mind that I'm about to get into an Uber."

"I don't mind, and please, call me Max. I'll text you a Zoom link. It will be me and a few other involved parties."

The link comes immediately, as does my ride.

As soon as I'm situated in the Uber, I get on the call, which turns out to be an interview. And despite what happened with Michael earlier, I manage to answer every question calmly, describe the show that I'd create without any hesitations, and overall project a professionalism and confidence that I do not even remotely feel.

"That all sounds good," Max says, speaking for the whole group. "Now, let's talk about your compensation." He throws me a number that is triple what I currently make—even with the incentives to pretend to be dating Michael.

Unable to believe that I'm actually doing it, I counter with a number that's fifteen percent higher, and Max agrees.

"In that case, I'll take the job," I say giddily.

I would have taken it even with a pay cut, but I'm glad they don't know that.

"Perfect," Max says. "Can you start tomorrow?"

"Tomorrow?" I swallow as the enormity of what's happening finally hits the lizard part of my brain—and is maybe making me hear things.

"I know it's a Saturday," he says. "But the theater is open."

"But… tomorrow?"

"Right. Sorry, I neglected to mention the urgency. The reason we have an opening right now is because another theater poached one of our performers. My wife reminded me of you, and you were the first person I called."

The first person… but he's got more on his list? "I have to give my current employer two weeks' notice." At least I assume that's what they would want. They never really discussed that with me, just the fact that they'd fire me on the spot if the old mascot, Ted, reappeared. Speaking of Ted, he just stopped showing up for work one day, and the team was fine. Then again, Ted wasn't pretending to be dating one of the players.

Shit. I obviously can't *pretend* to date Michael now that we've actually started dating. And have just imploded. With that in mind, two weeks of bumping into him sounds like torture. But still—

"You're a mascot," Max says. "Your face isn't seen. The team can replace you in a heartbeat."

Mean, but true. They hired me the next day after

they decided to fill Ted's position, and I was one of twenty applicants.

"But… tomorrow?" I won't even get a chance to see my family before I go, or—

"Look at this from our perspective," Max says. "Even if you arrive tomorrow, you'll need to rehearse and prepare, so we'll already be losing a couple of weeks' worth of earnings."

More like a month or more if we're realistic, but I don't point that out because I don't want to lose this opportunity.

"Just to clarify, are you saying you will not wait?" I ask.

It sounds insane, but then again, the rush does solve a question I haven't dared to ask myself: where should I stay tonight?

It can't be Michael's place. Not after—

"Sorry to pressure you like this," Max says. "We'll cover all your travel expenses, including an airplane ticket for tonight and a hotel room near the airport. Then you can stay at the—"

He goes into more details, but I only half listen.

I always thought that when I got the job of my dreams, I would be beyond happy, but depressingly, that's not how I'm feeling at all.

Instead, I'm numb. The seesaw of losing Michael, followed by this interview, is just too much to process in such a short time.

"How does all that sound?" Max asks, bringing me back to the conversation.

"Great," I reply, imbuing my voice with the cheerfulness that would be there had everything not gotten so messed up. "I will see you tomorrow."

With that, I hang up and face Wolfgang. "Can you believe it? We're going to have our show, after all."

He rubs his paws on his face.

Meine Liebe, can my stage name be Das Cheese?

CHAPTER 24
MICHAEL

A Ford Mustang Shelby GT500 can reach 180 miles per hour—a speed I hit at least a couple times in my haste to get to the stalker's house.

A stalker who's turned out to be my fucking teammate, of all people.

Burning tires as I come to a screeching halt in front of his house, I leap out of the car and smash my fist into the door.

"Who is it?" Jack calls from the other side.

Yes. It's fucking Jack, a fact I never would have believed if it weren't for the security footage.

I didn't think he'd have the balls to mess with my woman.

Balls that he's about to lose.

"It's Michael," I reply as calmy as I can, which isn't very. "Open. Now."

I fully expect him to realize why I'm here and refuse

me entry, which would be fine, because it would be my pleasure to break his fucking door down.

But he does open the door, and as soon as I see his face, I plant my fist in it.

With a pained grunt, Jack collapses on the floor, and I raise a leg to kick him when I hear a muffled sound from inside the house.

It sounds like someone screaming, "Help!"

"Who is that? Is that the last person you stalked?" I demand from Jack, but he's still on the floor, moaning as he cradles his jaw.

The plea for help repeats, and the voice sounds vaguely familiar.

"Stay here or you're dead," I growl at Jack, then sprint inside, following the voice.

It takes me a few minutes to figure out where the sound is coming from: a padlocked room at the back of the house.

I tug at the padlock, testing its strength as I yell, "Hey! Who's there?"

"Medvedev, is that you?" The voice sounds even more familiar now, though I still can't place it.

"Yeah, hold on!"

The padlock doesn't give, so I scan my surroundings until I spot a key on the nearby coffee table. Grabbing it, I unlock the door and finally recognize the speaker.

It's Ted, the guy who was our mascot before Calliope got his job. He's unshaven and filthy, but it's definitely him.

Wait a second.

The reason we needed a new mascot was because

Ted disappeared without a trace. Is this where he's been?

Judging by the looks of him, it's pretty likely.

But why?

Does Jack have some weird obsession with whoever is inside that bear suit? Is that why he shredded it in our hotel room?

"What happened?" I demand, glaring at Ted. "Why did the fucker lock you in here?"

Ted scans the room, wild-eyed. "Where is he?"

Oh, shit.

I run back toward the front door.

No Jack.

"Fucking shit." I return and grab Ted by the shoulder. "Help me catch the fucker."

We run out of the house and search a couple blocks, to no avail.

"Get inside the car," I order Ted when we're back at the house. "We're going to drive around looking for him."

Ted obeys, and we circle around the neighborhood, but with zero results.

Fuck. Where could he be?

Shit. Could he have gone after Calliope?

Everything inside me goes cold.

"Buckle in," I growl at Ted and floor the gas, heading back to the circus.

"Where are you going?" Ted gasps as we blow through one intersection after another at breakneck speed.

My jaw flexes. "He might be after my girlfriend. She's the new mascot."

"Huh," Ted says dumbly. "Why would he be after her?"

"For the same twisted reason he locked you in that room?"

"Oh?" Ted looks confused. "Did she also take a video of him jerking off to that gator?"

His question is so confusing I actually have to slow the car. "What the fuck are you talking about?"

"That's why he wouldn't let me leave," Ted laments. "We got high together, and when he thought I was asleep, he snuck outside. I followed and caught him standing by the lake with his dick out. He was staring at the gator as he was jerking off and grunting shit like, 'Yeah, those teeth. Those scales. That fat, juicy tail…'"

I glance at him incredulously.

Is he shitting me? I get that this is Florida and all, but come on.

"So… you see a dude jerking off to a gator, and your first reaction is to take a video of it?"

"I was high, dude. And it was funny as fuck. But Jack saw me filming him. He seemed crazed, so I jumped into my car, went home, and stuck the footage on a USB flash drive. I then texted Jack to tell him that if he came after me, or if he pissed me off in general, I'd mail the flash drive to WTVJ." Ted rubs his nose. "The next morning, he knocked me out as I was leaving my house, and then he kept me locked away until I told him where 'all the drives' were. He didn't believe that I only had the one, stashed under a floorboard in my place. So I was stuck. Thank God that you came over when you did. I was about to go insane."

Fuck. Suddenly, everything clicks into place. Calliope was right when she thought someone had snuck in and looked under the floorboards in her—formerly Ted's—place. It was Jack, looking for the only existing flash drive. But Jack must have thought—and I use that term loosely—that Ted had hid another hypothetical drive in his bear suit, so he kept coming after it, first in Calliope's dressing room, then in the hotel. I bet that's why he tricked me into pushing her in the pool while she was wearing the suit for the first time—in the hopes that the drive would get damaged. Or that she'd leave the suit drying, and thus unattended.

What a fucking idiot.

Correction: idiots, the both of them.

"Can you do me a favor?" Ted asks plaintively.

I grit my teeth. "What?"

"Can you take me to the sheriff's office?"

I'm about to tell him, "Fuck, no," because I have to save Calliope, but then I realize Ted's story means she's not in any danger from Jack. Or from any stalker.

She never was.

I should be ecstatic about that, and I mostly am, but a part of me is disappointed as well. Without the danger, there's no reason for Calliope to stay at my place anymore. Not unless—

"I really want to file a report," Ted says pleadingly. "And get a restraining order against that asshole."

Fucking fuck. "Fine. But you owe me, big."

If cops are involved, I'm not going to be as free to

enact my revenge on Jack, but then again, getting arrested and having the ridiculous story Ted just told me become part of the public record is a cruel and very unusual punishment in itself.

I can see it now: "Florida Man masturbates to gator, then kidnaps hockey team mascot."

———

To my shock, there's not a hint of mirth on the sheriff's face as Ted rattles out his tale—as though shit like this happens here all the time.

"I need to get back to my dinner," I tell everyone before the sheriff asks who I am and what my role is in this whole mess. The last thing I want is to get delayed for however long it'll take Ted to file an official police report.

"How am I going to get home?" Ted whines.

Should I tell him his "home" was given to someone else?

Nah.

"How is that any of my fucking business?" I demand.

"It's fine," the sheriff says. "We'll give him a ride."

Whatever. I run for my car and return to the circus, eager to tell Calliope the whole story. To my relief, the dinner is still ongoing, but Calliope is missing from her seat.

And her family is staring daggers at me over their dessert.

Shit. For the first time, I realize that I left rather abruptly, likely offending them.

"What are you doing here?" demands the trapeze sister.

Fuck. I did screw up. "Sorry, I had to leave on important business. But I'm back. Where's Calliope?"

The sister scowls at me. "Did you explain your 'important business' to her?"

Double fuck. "I was in a rush to resolve the issue that arose."

And by "resolve," I mean "break some bones."

"Well, then, you messed up, big time," she says. "My sister thought you hated our family."

"Hated your family?" I look around. "The opposite is the case."

"The opposite?" She arches an eyebrow. "That would be loving the Klaunbuts, and that's a tough sword to swallow, even for Uncle Bruin."

"Trust me," I say earnestly. "For someone whose family abandoned him, seeing how much you all care for each other is a revelation." And as I say the words, I realize that they're true, and so is something else.

I don't just love the Klaunbuts' family dynamic. I may actually love one Klaunbut in particular, which is insane, given how—

"Then you'd better go after her," the sister says. "And hurry."

Fuck.

She's right.

As I run back to my car, I call Calliope, but she

doesn't answer. I text her as well—but I don't get a reply, which isn't a good sign.

Leaping into my car, I floor the gas once more, and a few minutes later, I approach my front door... only to catch Calliope stepping out with her suitcase and rat carrier.

Something in my chest shrinks, like a punctured tire. "You're moving out? Just like that?"

I know I shouldn't really be surprised, not after all the other people who abandoned me in my life, but this is on another level. Calliope doesn't know that the stalker situation isn't a problem anymore—which means she'd rather be in danger than spend another minute with me.

"Of course I'm moving out," she snaps. "I can't be with someone who hates—"

"Don't say that I hate your family. I never fucking said that."

"You didn't have to. Your actions spoke volumes."

I take in a calming breath. Maybe if I explain it just right, she won't abandon me. "I didn't leave because I hated your family. I left because I learned who the stalker is—and it's someone I know. I got very angry and rushed to deal with him. In hindsight, I should have told you, but—"

"You learned who the stalker is?" Her eyes are wide.

I clench and unclench my fist, sorry that I punched him just once. "Yeah. It's Jack."

She blinks at me. "Kangaroo Jack?"

"Kangaroo?" Now that she mentions it, Jack does vaguely resemble one. "Yes. That Jack. As it turns out, he wasn't after you. He was after a flash drive that has a recording of him jerking off to a gator."

Her eyes narrow. "You think this is a good time for a joke?"

"I'm not joking," I grit out. "Ted—whom Jack kidnapped—hid the flash drive in his apartment, which then became your apartment, hence the moved floorboards."

At this point, her eyes are mere slits. "You expect me to believe that horseshit?"

"Why the fuck would I make this up?" Taking another calming breath, I add, "Ted is filing a police report. They're public record in Florida. You can check."

She grips her suitcase tighter. "Fine. If that insanity is true, I don't have a reason to stay here anyway."

I gulp in the next breath, and it's anything but calming. I force the next words out. "Don't go."

She swallows, and her gaze drops to my chest. "I… kind of have to."

"What do you mean? I'm telling you, the stalker situation is over." Once more, I force myself to say the words that I never got to say to my parents. "I want you to stay. With me. I know we've only been dating for—"

"Less than a week." She takes a deep breath herself. "This is too soon for a step like moving in together. But more importantly, I… accepted a job offer. In New York."

A puck smashing into my gut would be less painful than this. "You did what?"

She steps back. "I thought you'd broken up with me.

I thought you hated my family. And this is a job I've always wanted."

"What job?"

As she explains, I feel nausea coming on—no doubt I've become carsick from driving like a maniac.

"I see," I say when she reminds me that the rat show has been her dream for as long as she can remember. My tone is hollow as I say, "In that case, you should leave. Now."

She rushes past me and gets inside an idling Uber.

My nausea worsens as I watch the Uber pull away and disappear from sight.

Turning toward my front door, I smash my fist into it, over and over, until the wood cracks and the pain in my knuckles distracts me from the turmoil in my mind.

The reprieve is short, however.

I soon recall what a fucking idiot I've been.

Why did I ask her to stay? Why did I think it would make a lick of difference?

I should have fucking known better. Nobody has ever stayed for me.

Not. A. Single. Soul.

CHAPTER 25
CALLIOPE

I cry the whole way to New York, which is stupid, because I should really be ecstatic—I've gotten the opportunity of my dreams.

As the cab takes me from the airport to the hotel, my phone rings, and my treacherous heart speeds up, hopeful to hear Michael's voice.

Nope. It's Seraphina.

"Hi," I say, doing my best to sound cheerful.

"Did Michael find you?" she says instead of a greeting. "He came back to the cafeteria and—"

"Yes, he found me." For all the good that it did.

"And?" she demands.

"And we broke up," I say, fighting a hiccup.

"Why? Didn't he explain? He—"

"Left on some urgent business. He told me. It was too late, though."

"What? Why?"

I take a deep breath. "I have amazing news. Should

have started with that, actually. I got a job in New York. I'll have my own rat show. Like I've always wanted."

There. Saying the words makes me feel a tiny bit of the excitement that I should've been feeling this whole time.

"Wait. Back up," Seraphina says. "How did that happen?"

I tell her, and feel like a traitor when I get to the part where I met my new employer during an event that Michael dragged me to.

"This is amazing," Seraphina says when I finish. "But what about your Boo? Why the breakup?"

I shrug, then realize she can't see me. "He wanted me to move in with him. This job means I can't."

"But you'd already moved in," she says.

"That was for protection. This would've been for real."

"And you said no?"

I bite my lip. "I did. Because of the job."

"So… you're going to do long distance, right?" she demands. "Or something?"

"I don't think so." Given his expression as I left, I doubt he'll ever talk to me again. "And it's for the best, really. I realize he didn't leave because of our family, but I bet he hated us anyway." Like all guys do.

"Wrong," Seraphina says. "He told me he loved our family. Said something to the effect that he likes how we all care for each other." She pauses. "Are you sure you're not projecting issues with all your exes onto him?"

I narrow my eyes at the phone. "Why are you taking his side?"

"What? I'm not."

"Why not congratulate me for getting the job? Why not tell me I'm better off without him? Why not—"

"Look, I'm not the one you're mad at," Seraphina says.

"Don't tell me whom to be mad at."

"You know what? This conversation is over," Seraphina says. "Call me when you're ready to apologize."

I'm about to counter with something along the lines of that happening on one chilly day in hell, but she already hung up on me.

Asshole.

I fume all the way to the hotel, then drag myself out of my funk by rehearsing an actual show with my rats —an activity that makes me feel a tiny bit better. But not that much.

The next day, the first thing I do is call Linda from HR, but then I recall that it's Saturday and hang up. To my shock, she calls me back, so I apologize profusely for the short notice and give my resignation.

"That saves us from making a difficult choice," she says.

"Oh?"

"Ted is back," she says. "And it turns out that missing work was beyond his control."

Ah. Right. So that part of Michael's crazy story is true.

"Great," I say. "Glad you don't have to fire me."

"I didn't say we were going to," she says. "You did us all a huge favor with the 'Honey and Boo Boo' business, so—"

"That's over also," I say.

There's no way Michael would be willing to pretend to be with me, and vice versa.

"PR will be disappointed, but I completely understand," Linda says. "Best of luck to you with your future endeavors."

I thank her and hang up, somehow still feeling guilty for ditching the hockey team like this. No goodbye to Coach. No sayonara to Dante or any of the others.

Shit. I haven't even told my parents about my move —though telling Seraphina means they know by now. My sister is like a Klaunbut internet.

Still, I call to tell them officially, and my heart squeezes when they tell me how happy they are for me.

"So sad about Michael," Mom says just as I was about to tell her about that part. "Your sister told us you broke up."

"Yeah," Dad says. "I liked him a lot more than What's-his-face."

What's-his-face is what everyone calls most of my other exes, and I think it's because the dislike was mutual in those cases.

"I have to go," I say, not ready to discuss Michael.

"Sure," Mom says. "Break a leg."

I hang up with a smile, which turns into a frown as I check my phone for any calls, texts, or emails from Michael.

There are none.

Just as I thought. It's over. I'm never going to hear from him again.

Was Seraphina right? It's true that every boyfriend I've ever had dumped me after meeting my family. Did I break things off with Michael so fast because I was afraid it would happen again, no matter what he said about liking my family and wanting me to stay?

No. I did what I had to do. He's met them just the once, and he didn't even stay for the whole dinner. Who knows what would've happened if we'd continued with our relationship?

Actually, I do. He would've dumped me, like all the others.

It was just a matter of time.

Regardless, my chest is painfully tight as I head over to the theater, where I find Max waiting for me along with everyone else from the interview. There's also a large group of unfamiliar people who turn out to be theater staff and their families.

"We have a tradition," Max says. "Everyone gets to see the first rehearsal."

Wow. Good team-building exercise but nerve-wracking for me.

I set up the projector, get on the stage, and start with something easy: I dress the rats in cute outfits that have been waiting for just such an occasion and have them strut around like models on a runway.

The rats don't seem to mind the crowd watching us, which is great. The same can't be said for myself. I actually feel some stage fright even though this group is only about a tenth of the maximum capacity of the theater—not to mention, I've performed in a sold-out circus in the past and have been a mascot at a crowded hockey game.

I guess the fact that this is important is messing with my head.

But hey. Everyone cheers when the first act is over, and that gives me the confidence to proceed. I get the feeling that I'll be able to handle a bigger crowd—it will just take a little getting used to.

When I get back to my hotel, my phone rings. Just like earlier, my heart leaps when I think it might be Michael, only for it to dive in disappointment when I see that it's Seraphina again.

"Sorry," she says without preamble. "I should have congratulated you on the job."

"No. I'm sorry. I know you want what's best for me."

"Exactly."

"And this job is that," I say, wishing I felt as sure as I'm pretending to be. Refusing to give in to my malaise, I tell her about my first rehearsal, including the unexpected stage fright.

"Yeah, I wouldn't worry about that," she says. "You're a Klaunbut. No matter how packed the circus, we can swallow swords and stick our heads into a lion's maw. What's a little rat action compared to that?"

CHAPTER 26
CALLIOPE

Over the next month—not a couple of weeks, as Max had hoped—my rats and I are so busy preparing for our first real show I barely have time to mope. That is, I only cry for an hour or two daily, check my phone for some communication from Michael hourly, and see mental montages of us kissing under the most ridiculous of pretexts, like when I spot two doves sitting close together on a tree branch. Or when I see any kind of birds doing anything at all, even pooping on cars.

By the time my first show is about to open, I feel barely any stage fright, which is great. The rats kill it during the performance, especially with the unicycle sequence. After the show is over, the crowd actually rises to their feet to give us a standing ovation.

As I take my bow, I want to kick myself for not fully enjoying this pinnacle moment in my life. More than anything, I want Michael to be in that crowd. I want him to hug me afterward. I want him to—

Realizing I've stayed bowed past the curtain falling, I unbend, give my little guys amazing treats, and then go mingle with my family, who flew in for the show and sat in the front row.

"So," Seraphina says when we're alone together. "How bad was the stage fright?"

"Not bad at all," I tell her. "Go ahead and say 'told you so.'"

"Told you so." She grins maniacally, but then her expression turns serious. "Have you heard from him?"

I don't need her to explain who the "him" is in this scenario.

"No. And I didn't expect to." I hoped. And prayed, but—

"Have you called him?" she asks.

I frown. "Why would I?"

"Um, because you're the one who left?"

My chest tightens. "I did what I had to do."

"Did you? Why? Did you even consider the possibility of a long-distance relationship?"

The truth is, I didn't. At least not at the moment when Michael asked me to stay. Just minutes earlier, I was so sure he'd dumped me for the usual reasons that I couldn't fully process the fact that he hadn't. It's like my mental gears got stuck, and the only thing I could think about was that every other boyfriend had dumped me.

"You should call him," Seraphina states when I remain silent.

I swallow. "I don't think I could stand it if he doesn't pick up." Which he won't.

She frowns. "Why would he not pick up?"

"Why did he not call *me*?"

"Because you are the one who left," she repeats.

Damn her and her stupid good points. I know she's right. Michael asked me to stay. He said he liked my family, but I didn't really believe him.

Why didn't I?

Was it because every other boyfriend of mine abandoned me as soon as they met my weird family?

Or… maybe it's never been my family that they've found weird.

Maybe what really scared me was the idea that the weirdness they ran from was me.

"Seraphina…" My voice catches. "I think I screwed up. Like you said, he liked our family, and he proved that by asking me to move in with him. By asking me to stay. And what did I do? I left. I didn't even try to—"

She puts a hand on my shoulder. "Do you wish you'd stayed?"

I swallow the lump in my throat. "Yes. No. Maybe. You saw the show. I had to come here. But I wish we hadn't fought before I left. I wish we'd decided to make it work. I mean, I could have flown to Florida to see him every so often, and he could have flown to New York to see me."

In that moment, my brother joins us, so we can't keep talking about this.

Yet that conversation festers in my mind all evening and well into the night. The next morning, I wake up tired and heartsick but with an epiphany.

I can't go on like this anymore.

I have to try to fix things with Michael, and if he tells me to go fuck myself, that is a price I'll have to pay —but at least I will know I tried.

CHAPTER 27
MICHAEL

"You're retiring?" Dante takes his goalie mask off, blinding everyone with the paleness of his skin. "After all that hardcore practice?"

The rest of the team look just as shocked, and I can understand why. Lately, I have been a beast on the ice, but it was the only way to get my mind off Calliope. That, and I was doing Coach a favor by whipping the team into shape before departing.

"I've been increasingly focused on my foundation," I explain. "And the next phase will require me to travel all over."

"'All over' includes New York, right?" Dante asks with a wink. "After all, that's where Tugev—I mean, your biggest donor—resides."

"Exactly." Dante's Tugev jibe doesn't land because I no longer see that overconfident prick as an enemy. It's almost the opposite, in fact, thanks to a surprising number of things we've turned out to have in common.

"If I may." Coach slaps me on my shoulder. "You're going to be missed here, Michael."

"It sure won't be the same without you," Isaac says, and I can tell what he means is, "It will be so much easier for me to act in my role as the captain without an asshole like you undermining me at every step."

"Yeah," several of the players say in unison.

"And you can't leave until we have some drinks to wish you farewell," Coach adds.

This idea is met with cheers all around.

Fuck. At some point these assholes stopped hating me as much as they did before, and I guess I can almost stand having them around. Hell, I might even have to visit this shithole from time to time—purely because they are all sentimental ninnies.

"Can I have a word with you in private?" Dante asks, looking more serious.

I skate away, and when we're out of everyone's earshot, he asks, "When in the Big Apple, are you planning on visiting a certain theater?"

I give him a look so vicious he manages to pale another shade, which I didn't think possible, but here we are. "Go to the dick."

"Fine. None of my business. I get it."

He skates away, his shoulders stooped. Regardless, I want to give chase and punch his kidneys for putting the thought back into my head.

Not that it hasn't been there for over a month now, like a broken record. No matter how hard I've worked on the ice or how much progress I've made with the foundation, treacherous "what if" thoughts have kept popping up, like a splinter from a cheap hockey stick.

What if I'd left that dinner more politely? What if I'd groveled a little more before she left?

Fuck... what if I called her now? Wrote to her? Visited her?

Those last three are the killers, and it's taken all the willpower I possess to not give in to the temptation to reach out... and, lately, I've forgotten why I resist it so much.

Am I a fucking masochist?

My phone dings.

Oh, fuck. It's the guy I hired from a freelancer site.

I get off the ice, perch on a bench, and debate if I should watch the video that I commissioned. A video that is likely going to make the "what ifs" infinitely worse.

Fuck. Who am I kidding? My fucking excuse for willpower is useless. If it weren't, I wouldn't have hired the guy in the first place.

So, I play the video of Calliope's first show, and I'm glad that I'm sitting—and that I'm away from my knucklehead teammates. If my eyes are misty by the end of it—and they're totally not—the last thing I want is to have to kill anyone for teasing me.

Calliope was magnificent. She and her rats. And it was the first show. It's only going to get better from here. To be honest, I couldn't imagine the rats could be *that* entertaining, but they were, especially as they played their little soccer game, which has gotten a lot more sophisticated since I last saw it performed.

Fuck. I totally am a masochist. All the pain I felt when she left—it's back with a vengeance. As is the desperate desire to get in touch with her, or go after her, or—

You know what? Fuck it. I can't take this shit anymore.

I'm going to call her, and if she tells me to go to hell, so be it. I doubt I can feel shittier than I have this whole time without her.

Heart hammering viciously in my chest, I dial her number—and hear a phone ring near the entrance to the rink. The ringtone is *The Hockey Song* by Stompin' Tom Connors.

Weird.

As I wait for her to pick up, that ringtone keeps blasting. My chest squeezes when I get her voicemail.

Fuck.

I hang up and call her again—only to hear that same ring tone right behind me.

No.

Can't be.

Pushing to my feet, I turn around and frown.

The sound is coming from a person wearing some other team's mascot suit—or at least I think that's what it is. Then again, which team has a yellow bird for a mascot? It's got a giant head, enormous eyes, and clownish orange feet.

But wait.

On the shoulder of the bird… is that a rat?

"Calliope?" I exclaim.

The reply from the bird person is muffled, so I can't be sure it's her, but I step forward anyway.

The yellow bird lifts its arms and pulls off the giant head, revealing Calliope's beautiful face.

I gape at her. Is this a dream? "I was just calling you." I display my phone to her, like a moron.

"I saw," she says, beaming. "But I didn't want to spoil this." She proudly displays the mascot's head.

"*This* being what?" I manage to ask—even though what I really want is to sweep her into my arms and kiss the crap out of her.

Calliope frowns. "Isn't it obvious?"

"No?" I look at Wolfgang, hoping he can help me out, but all I get back in reply is a ratty chirp.

"I'm a canary," she says. "As in, *a bird*."

"Right…" I think I even recognize this particular bird now. It was in a cartoon, and there was a cat that wanted to—

"I'm your little bird," she says gruffly. "And you like birds. So, as my grand gesture, I used my old theme park connections to dress up like Tweety, who is the quintessential 'little bird.'"

Oh. "This is a grand gesture?" My heartbeat picks up. "As in… you want me back?"

She nods solemnly. "If you want me. If you forgive me." She takes a deep breath. "I'm so sorry about the way I left. I was so sure you had run from my family when you left that dinner, and even after I found out you hadn't, I just couldn't shift gears fast enough. All my exes had dumped me after meeting my family, and I was so sure you'd do the same that I couldn't entirely believe the truth when you told me."

"Calliope, I loved your fam—"

"No, listen." She sucks in another breath. "I realized that it's not really my family I was afraid you'd find too weird. Just like how, now that I think about it, my exes didn't dump me because of them. I mean, Voldemort petting her snake during dinner might've been the last straw, but the reality is, they dumped me because of *me*. Because I'm the weird one. I'm probably the Klaunbutist Klaunbut of us all, with my rats and my hair and—"

I capture her hand in mine. "I love your rats. And your hair. And all your wonderfully weird relatives." I mean, what the fuck is she smoking? She and her entire clan are awesome. Gruffly, I say, "And I'm the one who's sorry. I shouldn't have left that very important dinner with your family as abruptly as I did. If—"

"Stop." She squeezes my hand. "You don't need to say more."

"In that case…" I stop talking and kiss her fiercely, desperate to make up for all the time we were apart.

There are annoying cat calls in the distance, and even clapping.

Fuck. I forgot about my asshole teammates.

Calliope pulls away, glances at the ice, and blushes.

"Leave us!" I roar. "Or suffer the consequences."

To my shock, they *do* leave, but they laugh among themselves as they go, probably at our expense.

"Sorry about them," I say sheepishly. "Where were we?"

She moistens her pink, kiss-swollen lips. "I think

we're the ones who should've left, not them… so we can go find a bed."

And just like that, I'm harder than I've ever been in my life. But… "There's something I need to tell you. Something I should have said that night. Something that might mess things up again, but if—"

"What is it?" She drops Tweety's head onto the floor.

This is it. I'm getting a second chance at the biggest "what if" that has been tormenting me all this time.

I cradle Calliope's face in my palms. "I love you, *ptichka*." I stare deeply into her eyes. "I started falling for you when you took off that bear's head, and I saw your green eyes and pink hair for the first time. Then I fell a little deeper when you took off the gloves, and I saw your sparkly nails. And deeper yet when I saw the rat on—"

"Can I reply already?" she says with mock grumpiness, but her eyes gleam with happiness. At least, I hope that's what I see.

I nod.

"I love you too," she says breathlessly. "You're the drake to my duck and the dove to my pigeon."

Is my chest glowing? Because that's what this feels like. "You know, ducks are not the most romantic birds to use in your declaration of love," I can't help but point out. "They don't mate for life, and they have very aggressive sex." Not to mention an even less romantic factoid: drake dicks are shaped like corkscrews. "Oh, and a dove is not a female pigeon or vice versa, which you seemed to imply. They're technically the same bird, but with slight chromosomal differences."

She rolls her eyes. "I love you despite what you just said. I love you as if I were…" She pauses, searching for words. "As if I were the puck to your stick."

And in response to that brilliant analogy, I kiss her again.

EPILOGUE
CALLIOPE

"Thank you," I say to the cheering Estonians in their own—albeit broken—language. "And please, in the future, I hope you can find it in your hearts to treat rats with kindness."

With that, the curtain falls, and I give all my rats their treats, especially Lenin, who just executed a tight-rope walking routine almost as well as my grandmother would have.

Tovarisch, I can't believe you brought me to a country that dares to thrive after abandoning the glory that was the Soviet Union.

Gathering my things, I head backstage, where I meet some of the VIPs and give them my autograph—something I've been asked for more and more as of late.

When the signings are done, I approach Michael and a group of children that he's with, kids who are about to begin a career in a sport of their choice thanks to Michael's ever-growing foundation.

"Children, meet my wife, Calliope," Michael says

proudly. "Calliope, meet the children." He then presumably says the same thing in Russian, which is the most popular minority language in this country.

Using Michael as an interpreter, I learn all their names as they tell me how much they loved the show.

When the twins—a.k.a. two of my most favorite people in the whole world—join us backstage, Michael beams at them and says, "These are our children, Sasha and Filipp." Just like earlier, he repeats the whole thing in Russian.

His protégés look at the twins with unabashed curiosity, and a girl says something to me in Russian that Michael translates to be, "You seem too young to be a mother to such big kids."

That's not true. The twins are nine, so I could've given birth to them… in theory.

Michael gives a whole monologue in Russian, one where he probably explains that Sasha and Filipp are biological brother and sister, and that we met them at a Russian orphanage and adopted them soon after.

Hopefully, he does as I asked him and skips the bit where his foundation couldn't help the twins because they weren't into any sport. And that their story was particularly heart wrenching: their parents were fire-fighters who died in the line of duty. And how the twins got bullied at the orphanage because they (mostly Sasha) had a pet rat, Lariska, who is now also part of our household.

"Mom," Sasha says. "Can I show them our rats?"

I smile. "Of course, sweetie."

Sasha chirps to her new friends in Russian and hurries away, her brother and the other kids on her tail.

Michael tells one of his employees to keep an eye on the kids, and then he asks me what I thought of the venue.

"It was amazing," I say. "Tell Mason—I mean 'Tugev'—that I owe him a huge thanks for suggesting we tour his fatherland."

"I will do no such thing," Michael growls. "The fucker's ego is already gargantuan; I refuse to feed it anymore."

Hmm. Speaking of things getting gargantuan...

"Boo," I say tentatively. "There's something I've been meaning to tell you."

He cocks his head. "Does someone else in your family want to adopt?"

That's a legit question because a number of my relatives have followed our example and given a home to some of the children Michael's foundation wasn't able to help. Not to mention, my family as a whole has fully adopted Michael with such enthusiasm you'd think playing hockey—or giving me orgasms—were one of the core circus skills.

"No," I reply. "But you're warm. This does have to do with an increase in our family." I put my right hand over my for-now-flat belly. "I'm officially a VIP lounge for a bean-sized hybrid between a clown's butt and a bear."

Shit. I shouldn't have made the bear joke at a critical moment like this. After I took the last name of

Medvedev, I decreed that I'm allowed to make bear jokes in lieu of the ones about clowns and butts, and Michael has been smiling when he hears some of them, but—

Michael grabs me in a bear-like hug and rumbles excitedly into my ear in a mixture of English and Russian.

When he finally releases me, his eyes gleam. "I didn't think I could feel feel *this* happy at the news. Thank you, *ptichka*."

"Thank you?" I roll my eyes. "Save the thanks for after the bean—which will be the size of a small pumpkin—comes out of my pink panther."

He nods gravely. "I'll thank you when that happens. And I'll thank you *now*. And I'll thank you every step of the way."

My lips quirk. "The best thanks would be a foot massage."

"Consider it done."

I grin. "What about homemade *vareniki* with mushrooms?"

"I'll make them anytime you have the craving," he promises. "Other stuffings too."

"Speaking of stuffing," I say. "There's one more thing."

He arches an eyebrow. "Yes?"

"In one of her TMI vomits, my mom told me that all the women in our family have an increased sex drive while preggers."

His nostrils flare. "Increased? Beyond what it is now?"

I lightly punch his chest. "If that happens, I want you to—"

"Make you come, over and over," he says huskily. "And then come some more."

"That sounds good," I say breathlessly. "Let's shake on it." I extend my hand.

He takes the proffered hand and gently caresses it. "I have a better idea." He pulls me in and whispers, "How about we go to your dressing room and get the ball rolling on all this gratitude?"

I clasp his hand tightly. "I thought you'd never ask."

With that, we seclude ourselves, shed our clothes, and Michael proceeds to demonstrate for me the kind of care I can expect for the rest of the pregnancy.

And for the rest of my life.

SNEAK PEEKS

Thank you for participating in Calliope and Michael's journey!

Curious to read the story of Michael's nemesis, Mason? Check out *Pucking Billionaire*! Star hockey player Mason Tugev is nearing retirement, and he's faced with one major problem in buying his beloved team: the charming yet fiercely stubborn new owner, Sophia.

Love a Florida romance? Read *Billionaire Surfer*! It follows Brooklyn, an overworked single mom in desperate need of a vacation, and Evan, a billionaire surfer who, like the ocean waves, might just sweep Brooklyn off of her feet.

To make sure you never miss a release, sign up for the newsletter at <u>mishabell.com</u>.

Turn the page to read previews from *Pucking Billionaire* and *Billionaire Surfer*!

EXCERPT FROM PUCKING BILLIONAIRE

BY MISHA BELL

Sophia

Unexpectedly becoming an heiress should've made all my problems go away, but instead, I have three new, huge ones: two giant tortoises and a lean, mean two-hundred-pound hockey player named Mason. He's as hot as he is insufferable, and he would've made a fine Viking if he hadn't been born in the wrong century.

He wants to buy my hockey team, won't take no for an answer, and is willing to do anything to get his way… no matter how dirty he has to play.

Mason

All I wanted was to buy my team, but what was supposed to be a simple business transaction got complicated, fast—and all because I accidentally insulted a woman who turned out to be the new owner… and a force of nature. Now all my carefully laid plans are unraveling, and I'm faced with a life-changing choice.

Do I still want the team, or do I want the team's owner more?

———

Still in a daze, I scan my surroundings.

There are two men waiting here: a mustachioed, portly one reading a magazine and playing with the buttons on the collar of his shirt, and a tall, broody, broad-shouldered specimen who is clutching his phone in a tight fist.

Oh, boy.

That fist.

Not this again.

But yep. There I go, turning wet, hot, and bothered at the mere sight of it.

What is wrong with me? You'd think after all that I've just gone through in that office, sexy times would be the last thing on my mind, but it seems like the stupid fist thing is never turned off.

In reality, I'm a peaceful person—a pacifist, in fact—and I'm not particularly kinky as far as I can tell, so I don't have a clue why the sight of a man's fist does to me what Viagra would do to a horny male teen. Oh, and the fist being attached to a gorgeous man like this makes the situation infinitely worse.

The guy has piercing gray eyes, a strong—albeit previously broken—nose, a powerful jaw, and eyelashes

I'd sell my soul for. And for some reason, he's wearing a track suit, which should make him look like an old-school rapper or mobster. To my eyes, however, he resembles a Viking. Maybe it's the longish blond hair? Or the fierceness he exudes?

If we're asking random questions, how does attraction actually work? Is "being hot" objective or subjective? Do we all have a choice in who we find "hot," or is this just another way to phrase the question about free will?

Whatever. I swallow the excess liquid pooling in my mouth and wish there were a pussy equivalent to swallowing. Just like with fists, despite loathing violence and everything else that Vikings represent, I find them infinitely fascinating. And I'm not proud of this, but I sometimes fantasize about what it would be like to roll in the hay with one... screaming Odin's name as I orgasm.

Fine, maybe I do have a kink. Or two.

"This is my lawyer's office too," the Viking growls sexily. "A stalker would wait inside her apartment."

Who is this "her," and why do I feel jealous?

"Oh, please," the Viking replies to whatever he hears on the other line, his gray eyes glinting with steel. "She shunned him all those years, but as soon as he got sick, there she was."

Wait a second. Is it my guilty conscience talking, or is he—

"You think she was interested in reconciliation?" he continues. "No fucking way. She didn't even come to his funeral."

Fuck. The brute *is* talking about me. But—

"All she wanted was the money, like a gold-digging vulture."

A gasp escapes my lips and all traces of arousal evaporate, leaving me drier than a prune in the desert.

The asshole Viking makes eye contact with me, and a rollercoaster of emotions flits across his features, not a single one of them guilt for what he said.

Mainly, he seems disappointed that he got caught.

Operating on pure instinct, I close the distance between us, poke his broad chest with my index finger, and hiss, "How dare you?"

———

Visit www.mishabell.com to order your copy of *Pucking Billionaire* today!

EXCERPT FROM BILLIONAIRE SURFER

BY MISHA BELL

An overworked single mom from New York City. A billionaire surfer from Florida. Can the turn of the tide bring these two together?

Brooklyn

Ah, finally a vacation. My son is at summer camp. My worries are back in the city. Now I just get to sit back, relax, and... get into a heated argument with my Airbnb host? Speaking of heat, is the Florida sun getting to my head, or is it the drop-dead gorgeous man in front me?

My friends did say I need some *Vitamin D*...

But my life is complicated, and no amount of adventure-filled treasure hunting, steamy make-out sessions, or ocean-deep conversations can convince me that our beach affair could last. Especially once Evan learns my secret.

Evan

I'm rich on paper, but I don't live my life like a typical billionaire. Nor do I date tourists. Especially ones who mistake me for a plumber and eat my breakfast before I have a chance to quell my hanger.

Brooklyn is argumentative, rude, stubborn, beautiful, smart, fun... Okay, let's say I kind of like her. That doesn't change the fact that she's only here for a week— or that I haven't told her an important fact about myself.

But if surfing has taught me anything, it's that you have to seize the moment before it's gone. And what if I don't want to let her go?

——————

On the flight to Jacksonville, Reagan plays his video game while I do my best not to snap at him or any other innocent bystanders. Thanks to my shit luck, the Red Wedding arrived mere hours ago, giving me the kind of cramps that, if you gave them to a prisoner of war, would go against the Geneva Conventions.

Thanks, body. Was a relaxing plane ride too much to ask for?

I glare at my wrist where my birthday gift from last year resides. It's an Octothorpe Glorp, a fitness tracker that's supposed to warn me when Aunt Flo is coming to town. Often, I imagine the gizmo talking back to me in a voice that's a mix of Richard Simmons and Gollum:

My dear Precious, if I could, I'd keep every tampon you've ever used in a shrine and glue to them the smiles I cut out of my favorite pictures of you. Alas, when it comes to the feature you mention, I merely track your cycles, not predict them.

I suffer the rest of the flight as stoically as I can. Once we land, I rent a car and drive Reagan straight to the camp—a beachy and chill establishment that plays Jimmy Buffett on a loop.

"Okay, bye," Reagan says without a second of hesitation before running off to check the place out.

I wait to make sure he doesn't run back and tell me he doesn't like what he sees. Nope. He probably thinks I've already left, or has forgotten that I exist altogether.

"He'll have access to a phone," the nearest Boy-Scout-looking counselor says to me reassuringly. "And we have your number on file. Once he's settled in, he'll give you a call. Go."

With a sigh, I head back to the car and start driving.

My mood was already crummy, but now it's worse than that of a stressed-out, sleep-deprived, and tick-riddled hippopotamus. The green and idyllic nature around me only makes me feel shitty about where I actually live, as do the much nicer roads and cleaner streets. But then I almost run over an-honest-to-goodness live alligator and feel a little better about the comparison between my namesake in NYC and Palm Islet, Florida, the illustrious little town where my vacation is to be. Same goes when a deer tries to commit suicide by car a few minutes later, and when the woman in the car in front of me stops to rescue a turtle —getting peed on in the process.

Got to love Florida.

My Airbnb turns out to be located in a gated community, and the female security guard at the entrance is as thorough as a TSA officer. When all my papers seem to be in order, she wrinkles her nose and mutters something about the HOA usually prohibiting Airbnb rentals in the community, and that mine is a rare exception to the rule. She further informs me that the HOA usually charges an overnight guest fee, but that the owner of *my* Airbnb is exempt from "all the rules."

Oh, the humanity. How do the poor members of the HOA sleep at night? As I drive away, it takes effort not to ask if the HOA in this case stands for Hilariously Overbearing Authority.

Driving through the community, I notice that the houses are charming mixes of Spanish, Mediterranean, and Caribbean styles, and that they all have impeccable lawns—must be the same HOA ruling with an iron fist. But when I pull into the cul-de-sac where my Airbnb is located, the monotone pattern is broken. Houses number four and five on Gatorview Drive are twins, and both have sharp corners, are covered in mirrored surfaces and tons of chrome, and remind me of something you might see in a modern art museum.

Since one of these is mine, I assume both belong to the same HOA rules-exempt owner.

My mood lifts minutely as I spot the lake adjacent to both houses, with untouched nature on the opposite bank. The view from my Airbnb must be spectacular, though slightly less so than from the neighboring house.

I check my fitness tracker for the time.

Dearest Precious ought to consider taking more steps, to tighten those succulent thighs for my stalking—I mean viewing—pleasure.

Crap. I'm too early for check in, and it's getting pretty hot. According to Evan, who's been sending me taciturn texts on behalf of this Airbnb, the code for the garage lock can only be used after eleven-thirty, but I may die of heatstroke by then.

Also, I kind of want the vacation to start, along with the associated relaxation.

Why don't I test said code now?

Walking up to the garage, I type in the code and the door opens. Score! Between this and the lack of a car in the driveway or in the garage, I'm pretty sure I can get inside the house.

After parking in the garage, I open the door to the house proper—which, according to Evan, is the entrance I'll use to come and go.

The door leads right into an ultra-modern kitchen the size of my whole apartment, and there, on the granite island, stands a spread of yummy tapas.

Now this is a fancy welcome. I spot a tiny piece of grilled salmon, a giant bean, a side of rice, an assortment of pickles, a ton of tiny vegetable plates, and something that looks and smells just like miso soup.

Japanese tapas?

Shrugging, I taste the salmon as I take in the lake view through a floor-to-ceiling window.

I'm jealous of Floridians yet again. In New York, you'd have to be a billionaire to have anything close to this house with this kind of view.

The fish is divine, so I sample each of the veggies, which are also amazing. Even the bean is tasty, and the miso soup is the best of its kind, sweet and savory in equal measure.

Suddenly, I hear rustling on the other side of the island.

What the hell?

The island is blocking my view, so I gingerly step over to where the sound is coming from—a sink that I couldn't see earlier.

I gasp.

A man is getting to his feet. Based on the tools scattered on the floor, I assume he must be a plumber here to fix said sink.

Now I'll admit, until today, if I were forced to picture a plumber in my head, he (is that sexist?) would look like Super Mario with a cartoonish mustache, coveralls, and as much sex appeal as a blobfish.

This plumber, however, has to be the hottest man I've ever seen.

His eyes are the clear blue of a Siberian Husky, his hair is the sun-bleached shade of a Golden Retriever's coat, and his sharp angular facial features are godlike with no dog analogs. Sadly, his ears are covered by headphones, but I bet they are sexy too. Oh, and his bare chest boasts an army of glistening muscles that include a six pack. Also, his nipples are hard.

Correction, it's *my* nipples that are hard.

Spotting me, he frowns, but he makes even grumpy look good. Then his gaze falls on what remains of the tapas, and his eyes beam icicles at me.

"Who are you?" he demands in a low growl that somehow manages to be sexy. "And why did you eat my fucking breakfast?"

———

Visit www.mishabell.com to order your copy of *Billionaire Surfer* today!

69113341R00150